PARDON ME

d.o. allen: Real Fiction.™ Really.

PARDON ME
and more suspense stories

TATE PUBLISHING
AND ENTERPRISES, LLC

Published by Tate Publishing & Enterprises, LLC
127 E. Trade Center Terrace | Mustang, Oklahoma 73064 USA
1.888.361.9473 | www.tatepublishing.com

Tate Publishing is committed to excellence in the publishing industry. The company reflects the philosophy established by the founders, based on Psalm 68:11,
"The Lord gave the word and great was the company of those who published it."

Book design copyright © 2015 by Tate Publishing, LLC. All rights reserved.
Cover design by Wendy Hibbard
Interior design by Gram Telen

Published in the United States of America

ISBN: 978-1-68142-296-1
1. Fiction / Short Stories (Single Author)
2. Fiction / Thrillers / Psychological
15.04.09

Acknowledgements

I enjoy writing and sharing each story with readers and listeners. Several people continue to be a part of this publishing effort. Thanks to Valerie Valentine for being the go-to person for critical editing. Wendy Hibbard, thanks for enhancing the cover design, and to Rob Stuttler, for the ideal photograph that captures the title character in "Pardon Me."

A special thank-you to the Tate Publishing team for ongoing support leading to this and a third book by **d. o. allen**.

It's real fiction. Really.

Contents

Preface

To each reader and listener—thank you!

With *Pardon Me*, you'll find another collection of realistic—but totally fictional stories. As with my previous book, *The Die*, you'll immerse yourself in tales that can happen to anyone while hoping they don't happen to you.

In my suspense stories, there are twists that will engage you and get you thinking. I trust you'll find solid, intriguing stories in this book that draw you in and still have you craving for more. You'll know where you're going in my stories but may be surprised at where you end up.

In this second collection, I keep asking, what if? In "Pardon Me," for example, what if a widow's conflicting emotions draw her dangerously close to her husband's killer? What if Shelby Ryle's aspiring rise to the top of the music world leads to a tragic rapid fall in "Backbeat"?

I've also included a story centered in the beautiful Lake Tahoe region, "Water Baby." One reader described it as "haunting and horrific." I was relieved when they followed with an enthusiastic "I like it!"

For those of you who are audiophiles, selected stories come professionally narrated. Vocal actors are matched with hand-selected original theme songs from outstanding singer-songwriters across the country. This gives you a listening alternative to traditional reading.

Thanks again. My stories fall like autumn leaves begging to be picked up. Thank you for picking up this book. More to come!

Backbeat

Shelby instinctively strums downward, her calloused fingers pressed on a fret of the weathered Gibson. Her artistic ode to lost love comes to a pleasant musical closure, echoing a calm finish to her five-song set at Nashville's renowned Blue Bird Café. With a wistful "I'm just another dreamer. Just another, just another dreamer," the song ends. Shelby flips her auburn tresses over her right shoulder with a practiced headshake, offering a demure smile. As the two dozen or so patrons offer polite applause, she accepts the polite, if not grateful, reply to her performance.

The ivory-colored guitar pick, her favorite, given to her by Corb Collins after his July concert barely a month ago, gets wedged into the strings. The worn instrument is placed in its battered case on the scarred oak floor of the modest stage. Shelby played Bird before, as had hundreds of singers and aspiring songwriters before her.

Most predecessors were forgettable names with self-scribed dirges or medleys of fabricated lovers. The lovers' names were not forgotten as they were never absorbed by the distracted listeners on some Tuesday or Wednesday night. Perhaps a dozen music performers here or at other local clubs were in the top echelon of the musical ranks. The morass of others kept their employment elsewhere, filtering to the bottom. Making a living off your hopes was brutal. As dreams evaporate, the image and echoes of each entertainer becomes very ordinary, fading quickly. Shelby had slipped in—not without considerable luck and inertia—somewhere in between the two extremes of musical acceptance. Recognized, though not well-rewarded, she is inching closer to a modicum of career soundness and is part of the Music Row's landscape.

Diners and drop-ins commonly approach her afterward to thank her, dropping a single or two into her open guitar case. Older guys—some double or triple her youth—are the most generous. With faces kind and sometimes weathered, she appreciates the twenties she sees some of them drop. The gents are nice, nothing inappropriate. Their words of encouragement are endearing. The mature crowd—even the couples—are the next most generous with tips. The dollars usually separate them from the floating fans: the ogling younger guys, studs, and an occasional female who always have a phone number on their mind when they step up to greet her. Shelby always politely declines. She wants a different kind of numerical offer, like a record deal.

Nashville, the Music City, radiates warmth. The metro's temperament remains from the decades preceding Shelby

Hess's arrival three summers ago. The climate is vibrant, even today. Several delete-clicks removed from being valedictorian of her Saget Sound High School in Seattle, Shelby ranked in her graduating class just about where the Alpha Placement put her when she accepted her diploma: somewhere in the sixty-fifth percentile. It isn't what it seems, she tried to explain to her mom. Shelby had the honor roll in her grasp a year earlier. Exceptionally bright, with complementary street smarts that served her well her final year in Seattle, the girl followed her passion rather than class ranking.

She nearly aced her classes for the first three years at SSHS. Her musical impetus urged her to step away from the pompousness of her classmates. Shelby began singing in local gigs scattered in the coolness of Seattle's oceanfront sound. Barely seventeen at the time, the talented musician solicited exposure at charity events, Catholic carnivals, and some local restaurant franchises starting her presenior summer. Shelby drifted away from her loose circle of teen acquaintances. In exchange, she habitually slipped into her shadow-filled house at two in the morning after playing compositions to a modest gathering at a neighborhood bar. She found it more comforting than rebellious or exciting when she slipped under the worn but clean sheets of her hand-me-down bed. The teen singer had a bit of Billy Joel in her, the eighties star whom her mom, Mary Ellen, had a crush on back in the day. Billy J from the musical belly of faraway New York City had built his career as a brilliant lyricist and piano player, slipping into nightclubs as a teen for both exposure and experience.

Billy's first hit was "Piano Man," a brilliant and poignant story of his early nightclub experiences. Shelby loved the song, sensing that she knows "John at the bar" and "Davey, who's still in the navy." Davey's probably retired now. The admiring fan smiled at her amusement. The hit song inspired her ever since her mom air-keyboarded the melody when Shelby was—what? Six or seven years old?

"Billy boy, you're old enough to be my grandfather, but you inspire me," Shelby invoked. Now here comes the chick with a guitar.

Senior year was a blur. Shifting to minimal maintenance with her schoolwork, Shelby saw her GPA slide from a three-nine to just above a C threshold. She was rarely showcased in the school's musicals or concerts. Perhaps it was the fatigued look in her eyes each week that led the music director to skip over her, choosing the more classically trained and scholarship-bound counterparts for concert assignments.

Shelby's body art did not help her image with school officials: a larger-than-life–sized kiss shape (now diluted from its once-vibrant red) layered over with a clef note. The musical symbol was black by intention; it remains a murky gray by result. The tat, visible on her front lower neck with most garments, was a gift from a bartender who took a liking to her a few months before her road route to Music City. She created the design on her own. Though she never had a neck kiss before, Shelby wanted to harmonize her love for music with a feeling of intimacy. She dreamt once—no, several times—that Piano Man, forever seventeen, planted the image on her neck, wet and sultry.

No sleep was lost over the high school's artistic spurning; she never colored inside the squares anyway. Artists never do. Instead, she turned her snubbing and isolation into the creation of musical stories. None of her compositions were self-revealing, but most had a solid basis of reality mixed with a strong emotional spice. Listeners found this mix alluring and appealing, and her lyrics matured over time. She was adept at taking her modest fan base into a reflective world of harmony and calmness with the birth of each new song.

Graduation brought with it coldness between her and her mom. Mary Ellen, age forty-two and widowed nearly seven years, had raised Shelby as best she could, only to see her daughter float away into music night after night. "Shelby," her mother would softly plead week in and week out, "you've really got to get ready for college. You can't just sit around in your musical fantasy." The mother supplemented her ineffective position by pointing out the names of several college-groomed musical successes, most of whom were born in time zones far different than Shelby's. "YouTube exposure trumps college," Shelby concluded, careful not to kick the blanket of civility off the bed her mom had provided. The ambitious musician wasn't rebellious by nature, just independent—and determined.

∞

With her mother's pressure abrasively rubbing her free spirit, Shelby enrolled at the local community college, hoping to get her mother to back off and that it would give her the opportunity to continue her gigs, authoring more musical nuggets between classes. Her academic act did not hold for long, and five weeks into the term, she quietly withdrew before the first grade reports went out. At two in the afternoon, following a fifty-five minute drone from a smoke-stained and overweight college prof, the disinterested student walked out.

Pulling together a few weeks' worth of clothes—mostly blue jeans and wrinkled, colorful T-shirts and tops— Shelby shoved her small cache of belongings into a canvas overnight bag with an airline logo on it. She gathered her wrinkled notebook of song drafts and a small scratched-up, two-hundred-dollar laptop. The modest hoard of personal belongings nearly filled the trunk of the twelve-year-old weatherworn Nissan Sentra. Carefully placing her Gibson in the small backseat, Shelby felt her heart thump as she closed the case lid over her musical friend. With the care of a doting mother, she looped the seat belt through the case handle and snapped the buckle into place, securing the guitar for the long ride. Glancing at her twenty-dollar-a-month cell phone, she typed in a text to her mom.

Sliding onto the dusty seat of the hundred-thousand-mile import, Shelby opened up the AAA trip ticket printed out the night before.

The Seattle clouds lingered at four-thirty in the autumn afternoon. With just a few hundred dollars of gig cash shoved into the glove box, Shelby turned the key, twisted the wheel to the left, and began the twenty-five-hundred-mile journey to Nashville, Tennessee. She was just a half of a mile shy of her nineteenth birthday.

Less than two hours later, a stunned Mary Ellen Hess sat at the kitchen table. Her eyes gazed again over the texted words Shelby had fingered into the phone: "I'll be fine."

∞

The former Seattle singer's first two years in Nashville were as pleasant as poverty allowed. There was a six-week stretch where she curled in the backseat of the Motel Nissan, the music in her head accompanied by the hunger growls of her hollowed stomach. Shelby sustained herself almost daily with just a ninety-nine-cent burger and a few swallows of day-warmed Pepsi from a nearby convenience store.

Her musical arrival into respectability was not due to a defined break, she thought, as much as it was an evolution. More like a sunrise that you miss because of being too busy; then a few hours later, it is seventy degrees outside and you suddenly realize how nice of a day it is. *That's what it is like*, she thinks. *A sunrise.* With this musing, Shelby realizes that the seed of another song is planted.

Nashville is bursting at the seams, sprawling some five miles beyond the concrete-and-grass perimeter of when Shelby first arrived. The city's venturing tourists assume it is polite to tip, presuming she is another starving musician who needs every buck she can musically play for. But she has evolved by catching on with two local singers, Corb Collins being one, who progressively climbed up rung by rung in singing popularity. Each can now claim to have a number-one hit on the charts. For Corb, it was an assurance of five years of bookings and shows as he cashed in on the success of his first smash, "Lonely Looking Back." The song is a legitimate hit that parlayed a hundred grand into his previously empty bank account. Shelby was given cowriter's credit, though she had only tweaked a line or two with Corb in the middle of his catchy chorus.

Mandy Clifford-Parsons is the other artist. With a well-developed gift for lyrics—though pushing the sideline of plagiarism—she scored with a self-penned ballad, "Quick Forever." Mandy's original composition was a blues-rock masterpiece but took off the charts when Shelby massaged the song into a slower rhythmic ballad. The emotion-invoking song peaked at number two in the adult-contemporary genre and garnered more than a hundred thousand downloads. With these two successes, the three rarely had time to appear at the smaller venues of Nashville.

Mandy, ten years older than Shelby, and with entertainment seasoning, brought the protégée along for a bussed concert tour, letting her sing backup during a tiring ten-city trip that just concluded in Raleigh. Mandy, though arrogant as hell, was at least generous with dollars and had given her backup vocalist a ten-thousand-dollar check for pitching in on "Quick Forever." In Music City, USA, hundreds of song crafters claim to have written a number-one hit. Mandy's spin of another composition, "City Girls and Country Curls," made it to numero uno on a national satellite station, enough to add to her resume, Number-One Hit Single. Shelby's name was not listed as cowriter. Money talks, and egos walk, as far as Shelby was concerned. Two other hungry writers had contacted Mandy's agent, claiming a musical rip-off. Mandy was one to believe her own press releases, and to her, it didn't matter what the jealous claims were. She was able to breathe life into the song to make it large enough to be successful, her name embossed with the song's copyright logo.

Not financially set by any means, Shelby's physical hunger was gone at least, and she secured the funding to purchase a modest condo in nearby Whitehouse, Tennessee. She was gaining recognition as a songwriter on the rise. An evolution is what it is, an evolution.

Eager to return home, she gathers up her guitar, not bothering to pay attention to the loose cash within the case or the hastily written and crumpled note on a paid receipt from the restaurant. Snapping the lid shut, she moves toward the exit and past a sullen man with an uneven suntan and an old University of Tennessee T-shirt. Thirtyish, he steps politely aside as she exits the Blue Bird. Shelby normally engages in at least a cursory hello, but it is eleven-thirty. She is eager to feel the soft support of her bed in the condo. She'd been on the road so long that she imagined a For Rent sign hanging on her bedroom door when she gets home.

∞

Stretching her back, Shelby blinks in the sunlight of the morning. She pulls an orange juice out of the fridge and rubs her dry eyes. She enjoys her healthiness now, sleeping within more traditional hours and wakening fresher each day so she can focus on writing. She did the two-in-the-morning lunchtime schedule when she first arrived, when she was able to text her few friends back in the northwest or to hang out in the clubs after she played. She's maturing, both in her music and in her lifestyle. Taking the advice of her mentors, including Corb, she learned to rest well and then start each day with at least thirty minutes of reflective storywriting or chord structure on her guitar.

In earlier times, those not so long ago, she had been awed by the legendary songwriters she had met. Most were wonderfully accommodating to her, sharing words of wisdom and experience. Oddly, there are no magic formulas for writing outstanding songs, though there are certain common denominators at the core of each biggie. These factors shift somewhat with changing tastes. Shelby still sketches out drafts on paper, which gives a more personal feel to each word as she writes on the pages of her finger-worn notebook. Her more mellowed writings go into the laptop, along with a melody draft and chord structure for the emerging song.

Shelby's library of self-authored music is up to thirty songs. Hundreds of sticky notes, scraps of paper, and even napkins hold brief references or ideas for future consideration. She enjoys the value of working words over and over, never being totally satisfied with her finished products even as she or others go to the studio to record. She is reminded, as one hitmaker had suggested, that great songs are not written; they are rewritten.

Squeaking the door open to her second-floor balcony, Shelby steps out to breathe in the cooled air of October. Beyond the flat pavement of the development's parking lot, past the highway signage of Veterans Highway, she can see the rolling countryside of middle Tennessee's Sumner County. Still showing the green remnants of the recent summer, she feels the urge to strum and sketch, pick notes, and write them down as well. Shelby wants to write, to play, and to create. She smiles as she remembers a quote from a million-record-selling songwriter she'd met following his appearance at a nightclub a few months ago. Making musical small talk after the final song, the writer said with a brilliant balance of tongue-in-cheek humor and mature seriousness, "I've always written hits." He told her, "I just didn't always have the *s* in the right place."

Humorous, poignant, and brilliant, thinks Shelby. *It's no wonder he's written such amazing songs with wordsmithing like that.*

Today is going to be a good day. Hits come from swinging, Shelby reminds her creative self. With that inspiring thought, she turns back onto the soft carpet of her bedroom and starts the familiar process of hot Starbucks energy, cutoff jeans, granola bar, and Gibson. Scrounging in a kitchen drawer, she finds the last of her nearly dry ink pens. She feels good; she feels ready. Today she's determined to put the *s* in the right place.

∞

Shelby strums and plays, pausing to jot down words, swapping the order here and there on her latest baby, "Sideways." She worked the song over and over in the past few days and, up to this point, had a pitchable hit to move forward to her network of singers. Usually avoiding the rigid grind of commercial music publishers, she prefers to market her own music, often playing new creations for the drops-ins on Music Row's many welcoming clubs and restaurants. She likes the feel of "Sideways," a song of someone who looks at things differently, from a different perspective, and who is comfortable in his or her own skin. Not unlike herself.

She strums the strings as she gently plays through the chorus one last time for the morning, pleased with the rewrite of the last verse:

> So I'll keep on resting, just prone here on the floor 'till
> I hear the creaking of another open door.
> Perhaps I will stand up since I saw the light. But I
> like my vantage point. So I'll stay for the night.

As a focused song crafter, she has a tendency to overthink, to imagine, and to act out certain parts of her songs. It helps to give her the feel and passion for each word as it comes from her lips. She feels her fingers move down the strings as "the clock blinks a number. Another minute erased." *Yes*, she thinks, *the do-over works*. She knows where the *s* belongs—right here beside her, though sideways. She senses the pride of another musical creation.

She lifts the guitar over her tied-back hair and kneels to place it back to rest. She realizes she never counted the tips (modest cash now, considering her recent success) and notices a scrap of paper. Not remembering that she scribbled down a hit tidbit normally reserved for her jeans pocket when the inspiration comes to her, she lifts the slip. The scratched words on the Blue Bird's customer receipt state bluntly, "Evil, a sin is alive. Your songs are alive. Someone will die."

The quick blank-out of Shelby's mind is shaken awake by the rapid thump in her chest. Her heart jumps to a high pulse, almost convulsion-like. *Sick*, she thinks, *this is sick*. Where did this come from? Who wrote it? Her memory draws back to the night before, to her singing, to her greeting of people afterward, to the U of T–shirt-wearing dude. Was it this oddly strange one who dropped something into her guitar case? He'd not asked her for an autograph. She remembers his sunken eyes, his look that seemed to laser through her as if he was looking at the wall behind her. His tainted teeth and week's growth of beard from last night's image gives her goose bumps.

She had heard stories of a few weird stalkers, of followers who pursue other singers like gum stuck to the bottom of a Reebok. Fortunately, she was spared this experience, and for the most part, the stories shared with her by Mandy or Corb had a certain humor to them. Corb had even named a pair who trailed him when he was in town: Twiddledee and Twiddledum. Corb, funny as always, seems to remember the fans back to a humid New Orleans summer show. The sloppy-looking couple had begun to venture way too close to the stage to be comfortable. Corb is always gracious with his fans, yet the name helps take the edge off the stress.

Corb joked it off, allowing Shelby to laugh at his description of the twiddle-twins' rambling but obsessed antics. They trailed him over the course of six Southern concert towns.

This is Shelby's initiation. A stalker. A prankster. A sick mind. *Evil*, the hand-printed note said. *Someone will die.*

Shuddering, Shelby feels suddenly chilled, like she had been tossed into the condo's ice-cold pool and she hadn't had time to dry off. She wraps her arms around herself to create some heat, but the note is creepy and cold in her hand. It reeks of tobacco. The slip of paper falls silently to the floor, but the words scream in her mind. *Evil, a sin is alive.*

Someone will die!

∞

Shelby's thumbs spasm as she taps a message to Corb. Two time-zone hours away, he most likely had landed at LAX by now for his appearance at an annual charity concert. Proceeds go to a pet-adoption agency that served much of Southern California. Shelby tries to clear her brain of the scribbled threat; nothing she does wipes away the words. She can't pass it off as a joke—a perverted one, if that's what it is—and she peels the mystery onion to see if perhaps it is a looming competitor or a jealous and frustrated singer trying to warp her psyche. Traditional law-and-order–type questions fire rapidly at her from a subconscious investigator: Do you know anyone who would want to hurt you?

No, she echoes.

Shelby completes her self-imposed interrogation, realizing that her creative bent to musical artistry fuels imagination and fears. Logic is a used chewing-gum wrapper in her front pocket and just as useless. The thought of Corb calms her to a degree. His steady, deep voice—so prevalent in his concerts and recordings—soothes her regardless of circumstances, real or imagined. Corb conveys wisdom with words carefully chosen to eradicate anxieties or stresses. His cooling voice wipes the trauma from her memory, a clean rag on a dry-erase board. She'll soon feel a smile on her lips as he garnishes his guidance with a bit of humor.

Craving a reprieve until Corb's response, Shelby taps on her computer and selects her most recent song draft, a still crude but promising third iteration. The soothing chords float through the air. The story of a young girl mourning the loss of her father reminds the singer of years past. Shelby's musical character is nameless but soulful. After tweaking several song titles, Shelby clicks "On A Day Like This." Reflective and transparent, the imaginary girl sits in a church and emotes to her now-spiritual father the agony of an enduring loss.

Shelby envisions a girl of sixteen, perhaps. As a writer, she struggles with the balance of musical raw emotions and a hopeful melodic closure. In her mind, scratched out as verses on several pieces of notebook paper, is a girl sitting on a pew in a small country church, praying while a candle burns atop a walnut altar. While the rhymes are still imperfect in the song, the emotional story is gaining maturity and artistic strength. She senses she is close to having the song into one in which she and hopefully her listeners are immersed.

A chime snaps Shelby from the musical fantasy back to now. Still not hearing from Corb, she responds to her phone's alarm that she is due at the recording studio in thirty minutes. Downloading the nearly finished composition, she reaches for her guitar case and heads out the door. *Evil is alive on a beautiful day like this*, Shelby muses. *On a day like this.*

∞

"Hi, superstar!" Barker Smythe greets her as she closes the scuffed studio door. Barker, a crude but lovable former Georgian, greets her with the enthusiasm of a rookie baseball player, never failing to bring a smile to her face whenever she enters the rustic fifty-year-old house on Grand and Eighteenth. What once were bedrooms now open to a boxy, padded, and wired morass of sound recording and enhancing paraphernalia. Some items are marred with memory but tried and true in capabilities. A few pieces—the mixer, for example—are costly and newer.

The house smells of music, technology, and nostalgia: the musical birthplace of fourteen number-one hits over the past two decades.

Barker falls into the grouping of marred with memory but tried and true.

"I was thinking we should do a track laydown for 'Day.' I've got the mix nearly done for 'Sideways.' I think you'll like it. By the way, when's Corb due back? He missed two sessions with his crazy schedule. Have you heard from him?"

"No," Shelby says, flipping the case open to retrieve her six string. "Corb's on the West Coast. Scheduled to take the red-eye back tomorrow."

"Weren't you working on a song for him? Something like a tribute song?" Barker asks. "I recall we saved a draft of it. 'Top Spot'? Was that the name?"

"'Top Spot,' you got it. I like what we did on it. The lyrics came together well, and the title has a hook to it." Shelby sits down on the all-too-familiar scuffed oak stool and tunes her guitar. "I'll start with 'On a Day Like This' and then we can do another run-through of 'Top Spot.' My hope is that both can be ready for release by the end of the month."

"You thinkin' of circulating them around? It worked for 'Quick Forever,' and Mandy picked it up," Barker reminds her.

Shelby paid her dues but still humbly knows the songwriter's maxim: her best song is the next one she writes.

She is committed to building her fan base and in releasing her own songs. Barker manipulates buttons and slide bars on a massive recording deck. A monitor flicks awake with the lyric images for "Day."

"I'm ready, Barker. We can lock this one in for mixing by noon and move into 'Top Spot.'" With her calloused fingers pressed against the fret, Shelby strums the opening chords. "Bark, let's make a hit song today."

Barker's headphones silhouette a Mickey Mouse shape. His graying and straggled hair falls against his rounded shoulders. A dilapidated T-shirt covers his ample belly. His arms are still parched from hours in the studio and too little play outside. Barker is part of the youthful crowd with his many nightshift sessions, going until three in the morning and then sleeping until nearly eleven each day. Shelby's arrival at ten is like dawn to Barker. In spite of his choppy lifestyle, Barker wears his sixty years very well.

∞

Driving down I-24, Shelby presses the tuning tab on her steering wheel. Pandora shares a soft green glow, "Shelby Hess Radio." The spring season is good for her, musically and financially. The seat of her new Maxima snuggles against her blue-jean pockets as she lets the sporty sedan find its way to Corb's house. Her mentor and friend is hosting a celebration for her newest hit, "On a Day Like This." Shelby feels the excitement chills on her sun-warmed skin. The song fills her car's interior. She is humbled but no less thrilled that perhaps thousands of others are also listening on Nashville's top country station, WNSH: the Big 98. Recent charting has the song at number three and rising on the country listings in downloads within three weeks of its release. The ballad just entered the top ten on the pop charts.

Corb is a benefactor, friend, and band soul mate. She is excited; her newly signed record label's new artist exec confided that "Top Spot" is to be released the first of May. Shelby is keeping the secret of this tribute song about Corb from Corb. Barker plays in on the surprise, partnering on the ruse. The name of Corb Collins, a major country star, is the hook of Shelby's newest musical creation. She ignores the satellite station now, opting instead to listen to "Top Spot" from Barker's superbly mixed final version. She loves—in a modest way—the three verses she penned. Barker added his masterful touch in the production of the song.

The Maxima rolls onto Corb's curved cobblestone driveway in the Nashville suburb of Gallatin. Home to several new-money music stars, Corb lives upscale but not pretentiously. The home is a classy five-bedroom brick and, as welcoming as he is, with landscaping that smiles at each visitor.

Corb's face is lacking its customary warmth. He walks purposely toward her, hands shoved deep into the pockets of his frayed jeans. Size-nine Reeboks scuff the stones as he approaches her car. Worry lines crackle his forehead. His family—two toddlers and a beautiful wife, Sarah—remain inside.

"Shelby, there's something you should know."

∞

Shelby sits on the web-laced chair of Corb's patio, her soul core stunned. Her mind is jumbled. Her emotions are now numb.

"I saw it on the local news. Then I followed up with an acquaintance of mine who's in law enforcement," Corb explains with as much fact-based compassion as he can muster. The now-weary singer continues:

"It was at the refurbished white church just inside of Hendersonville, on Old Main Street. The place has been around forever, but talk is that mostly just older people go there anymore. It's an active though quiet church. According to early reports, the girl was sitting at the front of the church. No one knows how long she'd been there or how she got in. Maybe with the church being nearly in the country, it was left open. Who knows?" Corb gathers his facts, at least those he understood, and slowly breathes out.

"The girl—reportedly a teenager—was sitting in the front pew. She was discovered by a custodian who came in to clean up following a funeral service held there the night before." Corb chokes up. "Shelby, she was found with a gunshot wound—fatal. She was wearing earbuds at the time of the shooting. I was told that she was found clutching a song sheet."

Shelby stiffens at the thought of where this sickening tragedy is headed. She can project the next words from Corb's mouth as he painfully vents the conclusion. Impulsively, she intervenes.

"Corb, please don't tell me…" Shelby spasms into dry shudders, too shocked to cry.

Corb stands chilled beside her, mustering the courage to conclude. "The song clutched in her hand, Shelby, was 'On a Day Like This.'"

∞

Shelby melts onto the bed, exhausted.

Corb had offered to drive her home following perhaps an hour or two of pondering, analyzing, withdrawing, and revisiting the news of the shooting. She had declined his offer, instead being drawn toward the shadowed reclusiveness of her own condo. Her arrival was greeted by another shock. Dropped at the threshold of her door was a used envelope, previously torn open and then stuffed with a handwritten note.

With hands quivering, Shelby unfolds the note. In recognizable text, the words she peruses through fear-blurred eyes: *Evil, a sin is alive. We panic in a pew.*

The agonizing letter ended with the words, *Amen, icy cinema.*

∞

The impact of the young girl's death reverberates throughout the Nashville region and hits CNN airways the following day. Shelby Hess is immediately associated with the teenager's ill-fated visit to the church. Though no direct link could be made with Shelby to the suicide, the event triggers landslide support for the girl's mother, who is now both a widow and childless mother.

The girl's name was Elle. Her funeral is attended by a wide range of well-meaning Nashville celebrities, most of whom were acquainted with Shelby's rising fame. The gesture is admirable and sincere as each fellow musician arrives to show compassion for the bereaved family and support Shelby's broken heart.

Now, senses Shelby, her image is but a tedious infamy and a public-relations disaster. The song crashes upon the news of the fatal shooting. Public outcry demands that disc jockeys pull the song from their playlists. The singer is not immune from sorrow. She grieves for the bereaved mother and funds a trust fund with ten thousand dollars set up in Elle's name.

Shelby shares the notes with the Nashville police detectives; Corb insists on it. *What would be next?* the grizzled veterans ask themselves. Budget curtailments prevent beefed-up security at concerts and major public events. Secretly, the law-enforcement establishment concludes that this is a one-time random event, and Elle's untimely death is determined to be suicide.

As an entertainer, Shelby is encouraged to continue her regional tour schedule. Gutting it out seems to be the only way. For the first time, she uses music as an escape from a troubled reality. Immersing herself into her songs, Shelby's record label approves the release of "Top Spot." The notoriety of the church episode dampens the impact of "Top Spot" on the charts, but it still sells a reasonable twenty-three thousand copies.

She and Barker continue to work on additional songs. Shelby pens a sultry update of an old draft, "Scars on Me," which Barker becomes enamored with. With a minor chord structure, upbeat tempo, and catchy beat, the song parlays the angst of a lovelorn teenager. While a capable writer, Shelby senses that some of her deeply buried emotions are filtering out within the song. A self-styled artist, she had not lived the life of a distraught teenager in high school. There were no missed proms, broken dates, and texting behind her back, or other traumas littering her background. Yet her sadness over Elle's death creeps into the emotions of the song. Becoming the key fixture in the song, whether by choice or not, sorrow adds an ingredient of sincerity to the song, hence believability.

Resorting again to scratching on a yellow pad, Shelby pens draft after draft, never disposing of the core of the chorus but exchanging, tweaking, and adding do-overs until she is reasonably satisfied. A ninety-five percenter, she accepts the standard that if she is 95 percent satisfied, then the song moves forward. The other 5 percent? Shelby attributes it to the indefinable pursuit of perfection. As a song, "Scars" stumps her. Thoughts on the third and final verse flash more quickly than her scribing of the words. Oddly, the song never clicks for her.

Shying away from time-weary references to a cold heart, to the ice inside your soul of another penned song, she probes for a fresh lyrical image. *How can I grab this thought?* she ponders. *How can I look at this differently, with another perspective, to come up with a refreshing but impactful closure to the song?*

Frustrated, she crumples another filled page of stale words and tosses it aside with the other litter of a songwriter. Taking an empty sheet of paper, she writes in bold grade-school font: *Scars on Me. Love. Cold.* She lays the fresh sheet on the floor, turning it clockwise in a moment of experimentation. A foolish act perhaps, but often, a new angle triggers unique thoughts that can spark creative lyrics.

Letting the discarded sheet rest, she writes again, striving for a crucial verse. "I lived out a fantasy, believing your hope." A blank. What did she cling to? A rhyme with hope. Rope. *Write it down*, she thinks. And she does.

Imagination comes to life as Shelby writes voraciously. "I lived out a fantasy. Not a bad dream, a nightmare." *That's where this song is going*. Bad dreams. Forget "Scars." It's "Bad Dreams." She held on to the rope. Both revived and inspired, Shelby masterfully writes on. While energized, she returns to the latest draft and scribbles in replacement words, knowing they are not discarded for good but placed in a junk pile for a future song. "Bad Dreams." A headache song, aggressive. She senses an ache in her temple. Writing can be joyous, and this one is a hammer that seems to pound inside her.

Time for a break, she thinks. *Aspirin?* Grabbing a plastic bottle from her nightstand, she is dismayed. Lonely Tylenol. One will have to do.

Her phone chimes, and Shelby hears it as a forgotten alarm. Two o'clock already. She was due at the studio with Barker, both eager to lay down vocals on a few rough songs. Maybe it's time to do a sing-through of "Bad Dream." Rough or not, structure sometimes comes through repetition. Grabbing her car keys, she takes up the notepad and heads out the door. Barker will be in full crazy swing now, having just eaten his noontime breakfast.

∞

Barker nods his head, murmuring to himself. His thick fingers toy with the keyboard. The visuals of the screen are familiar by color but not by pattern, and she steps closer.

"You're in a strange mood. What gives?"

"Hi, Shel. You know I'm a bit kinky when it comes to artistic exploration." Barker shifts in the tattered chair, moving his butt into a newly settled position. "I was screwing around with some tracks. Bits and pieces of what we'd recorded a few weeks ago. I was looking for a different approach to sounds, something fresh. You remember when you talked about laying a sheet of paper down, angling it, and looking at your writing? A different perspective kind of thing?"

"Sure. So what brilliant experiment is going to create a new hit for me?" Shelby humors him.

"The idea isn't new but is definitely experimental. Backmasking. Or a more sophisticated reference is, phonetic reversal."

"Backmasking?" Shelby recalls the term vaguely at best. Who knows, Barker may have told her about it. She didn't record a definition in her mental file, just the term.

Barker leads her forward, taking her gently by the arm as he stands up from the weary chair. "Take a seat."

The sound engineer rolls her up to the screen and clicks the mouse.

"Backmasking is replaying a musical excerpt, or any audible one, and getting a completely different message than the original. The concept has been around for years, probably ever since recording equipment existed."

She peers closer and places half of the headset up to her ear. "You mean like a palindrome? Where a word is the same backwards as forward? Like the girl's name Anna or even Hannah?"

"No, no, Shel. The opposite."

Barker relates the days before Shelby's birth when vinyl records were pressed and then sold as albums. The process is rekindling itself and is now once again popular with production purists and avid classic-rock listeners. Inside the studios, his being no exception, musicians and sound engineers once recorded on huge cumbersome open-reel tape recorders. Reel-to-reel recorders, as they were often called, were the finest recording tools available at the time of Shelby's grandparents, perhaps four decades ago, back in 1960 BC—"Before computers," Barker teases.

Continuing the historical lesson, Barker explains, "Take any lyrical portion of a recorded song and play it backward at varying speeds. The result, totally at random, is a new phrase or sentence. It's weird, man. It's like the joke of 'she said, he heard.' For example, we take a plug from a song. Let's say, 'Mary Had a Little Lamb.' Play it backwards on an old reel-to-reel recorder and maybe you get 'Eke is might time.' Or something crazy like that."

"I don't get it. Show me something." Shelby was intrigued but not committed to the time of this diversion. It wasn't the eighty bucks an hour he charged for recording time but rather his meandering away from her next song priority.

Barker explains to Shelby, "It's eerie. The music becomes distorted, almost surreal in its effect. Words to certain songs became ominous. Some people swear they heard messages. Original words played backwards came across as threatening—some claimed satanic."

Shelby finds this an intriguing but irrelevant history. To her, it is artistic exploration, nothing more. It was backward to her, like the label Barker placed on this musical oddity: backmasking. Barker explains that the alternative message was hidden or "masked" until it was played backward. Thus, backmasking was born and lived a fitful but short life when Barker was in the midst of his turbulent rock-music era.

"I know it was a lifetime ago, but you remember the Beatles, yeah, yeah, yeah?" Barker chuckles at his historical humor.

"Very funny. Yes, I've heard of them. Aren't they all dead now? Aren't they even older than Billy Joel, for Pete's sake?" She assumed they were all dead. What was it, fifty years ago? Suddenly Shelby is younger than her years. Was that her grandfather's era?

"Sorry, I forgot you're still a baby. The Beatles's biggest seller in the UK—before it became a hit in the US—was 'She Loves You.' Better known for the simplicity of the chorus, 'She loves you, yeah, yeah, yeah.'"

"Come on, Bart, get to the point."

"Sorry. The Beatles were known for creative exploration, perhaps originally discovering the concept of backmasking. Legend only knows. But one of the most famous examples is from one of their songs, "Revolution 9." Year 1966, I think. A line of the hit when played backwards, it sounded like…wait, let me show you."

Barker scrolls the mouse, reversing the colored slide bar on the computer. "This is the most well-documented cut, and it's creepy." He opens up a file within the system, and curious, Shelby lifts the phones to cover both her ears. She is now drawn into this musical though dated spectrum.

Twisting a volume knob slightly, he plays a loop that presents the same brief phrase four times in a row.

The first time, she admits, her mind had drifted. But the second play and the two following it are unmistakable in their clarity. Intrigued, she loops her finger in a circle. Barker complies and hits the repeat button. The scratchy-sounding voice did not vary from its first message. Shelby lifts the headset, springing the muffs away from her ears. "Wow" is her shock-delayed reaction. "Wow."

"Creepy, isn't it? I told you. But this is only one example. There were others back in the day. But this one was world-famous. Those of religious persuasion declared it was directly from the devil. Pastors across America, perhaps in Europe also, condemned the original song, claiming that the band intentionally was trying to get into the minds of teenagers worldwide to manipulate them."

"Now," he continues, "let me play you the original phrase from the song."

There was no question to Shelby, or any listener regardless of age or generation, what the song said forward or backward. She now understands the revelation of phonetic reversal: how a single, alternative message is heard from the original lyrics when played in reverse. The words came back in a crude form of English but discernable nonetheless. Backmasking.

"Turn me on dead man," said the Beatles.

Shelby's skin chills. "Turn me on dead man." Was it intentional? Just a random coincidence from musical experimentation? A thousand possibilities fast-forward inside her mind. She feels both interested and hesitant at the same time.

Barker, though confessing an uneasiness regarding the back masked message, takes a more pragmatic approach. "This is the shot heard 'round the world, Shelby. But I still think it's random. I don't see how this or other similar masked messages could be created intentionally. Not with the crudeness of recording technology of the times. We're talking the sixties and seventies here."

Shelby wants to move on, to wash this musical cut out of her mind. Like the song in her head in the morning, similarly, the "Revolution 9" blurb is the song in the afternoon etched into her mind: "Turn me on dead man." Sexual, it isn't.

"Bart, let's move on."

"Hold on, Shel. There's more." Barker enters a few more button pushes and recovers a musical file from her catalogue within the computer. "I just thought that you should hear this." He taps. With hesitation, she positions the headphones again. And she listens.

"Barker, how could you!" Shelby screams, grabbing the headphones and flinging them to the console. Stumbling over the chair in her rapid escape, the disturbed young woman flees the studio.

∞

No mere nightmare, the horrific musical message is still there when Shelby wakens just past three-thirty in the morning. Grateful she had made the drive home from Barker's studio safely, she could do nothing to expel the memory from her head. First came Elle's death, and now this? *Who is playing games with me?* Barker would never do such a thing. Perhaps he never meant harm but rather was trying to warn her. Regardless, she was fitful for the rest of the afternoon and evening. The forced two-mile run at a faster-than-usual pace didn't clear her thoughts. She couldn't concentrate to write or play any of her songs, even the standards of the past or her Corb creations. Tumult wore her to sleep about midnight. Then the awakening and the awareness that what she had heard was an actual event, it was also shocking.

She was torn between calling Corb or even Barker, but Barker was not the kind of insightful person who could walk someone through a tough spot. Besides, wasn't it his actions that caused this discovery? What did he do, just start replaying her songs in reverse until something jumped out at him? He certainly didn't imagine the eerie sounds. There was no mistaking the wording. Shelby heard it unmistakably. She struggled trying to sort it out, but she really needed to talk with Corb. He'd always had a way of soothing her with the ability to clear confusion up, a fog dissipated by the morning sunrise.

The burden is heavy, real, and disturbing. She reaches for her phone, sees the numbers 3:37 a.m., pauses. She opens up the contacts tab and scrolls to find Corb Collins. Consumed by uncertainty, she lays the phone back down, unused.

Amen icy cinema.

∞

"Shelby, I wish I could give you some answers, some guidance. This is too serious to just walk away from, too disturbing to ignore. Barker? What was he doing?" Corb spins his wedding band in circles as he ponders.

"What's gnawing me is that I can't dismiss it as a coincidence. All of the logic in the world still gets washed aside, and this phrase is etched into my mind. Nothing dilutes the anxiety, and I keep pressuring myself to forget it. But nothing works."

Corb's look conveys a false positive. His attempt to show his usual calm, pleasant demeanor seems stretched. Not fake but perhaps forced a bit. She trusts him immensely. Much of her career is fueled by his support and admonishments. He is her mentor. "Cheap sounds, Shel. That's all they are. With today's technology, you can create or manipulate anything. So it sounds like *amen*. And *icy cinema*? It's just coincidental muttering from a manipulated computer. Nothing more."

"So it doesn't bother you that is pulled out of my first aggressive song, 'Bad Dreams'?" Shelby hesitates to hear his response.

"Let's move forward. I'll ask Bart to delete all of his musical experiments with your song. We'll finish up the recording and release it. You're at the top of your game, and you've got to milk it while you're both visible and energized. Let's go." Corb talks as if he has already implemented the conclusion. His tone is more like a decision. He slides his chair back. The café is sprinkled with coffee slurpers, students, and a senior couple scratching on crossword puzzles. Their faces are relaxed; each is not burdened by backmasking.

∞

The Country Chord had opened less than a month ago. The do-over of the place is impressive: resurfaced floors with random-grained planks, a bar with brass step rails, and subdued but adequate lighting derived from discarded snare drums. Accents on the wall keep the musical motif.

Rope lighting is curled inside a dozen acoustic guitars and hung randomly along the dining area.

Corb set this gig up, which is not much more than a scheduled drop-in that Shelby agreed to less than a week ago. The Chord has trouble gaining traction with the extensive competition from three dozen other similar and more established venues. Singers, some who craft their own tunes, are plentiful. But the new owners stretched the remodeling budget. The drink options and snack menu aren't pulling in the needed funds. Corb knew the place previously as Lesley's, started and run for a few years by Lesley Peyton. Peyton had a dated but impressive image as a singer, garnering several award nominations before his propensity for white powder sucked away his creative genius. He died nearly broke. The spot had remained vacant until the new partners fired up the effort to reopen as the Country Chord.

Shelby and Corb penned out a set list. He offered "Let's Live" and an old dust-off—but one of his personal favorites—"Lifeline." Shelby's list included four songs, adding a rough version of "Make Up Your Mind" (her attempt at a humorous ditty) and her always popular hit "Just Another Dreamer." "Dreamer" was the first song she ever performed live in Nashville. Time proved it to be a winner.

She hesitates, starting to write *bad* then lifts her pen. Amen icy cinema. Amen icy cinema. She sees the words illuminate the page, threatening her from the song list. *Stop it!* she orders herself. Tensing, her hand cramps the pen as she scrawls "Bad Dreams" as the last entry.

She clips the list to a handwritten "Mind" lyric sheet and steps to the stage.

"Ready?" Corb's confident voice is cleansing. Yes, that's it—cleansing.

∞

The group of diners, flipping over laminated one-page menus, holds chairs by dropping purses or caps to save slots for friends, late as always. Word has it that Corb Collins is appearing, a local who had reached top-ten status twice in the last eighteen months. All it took was three autographed photos of Collins stuck to the front window of the Chord, complimented with the date and time in black ink marker. Crude, but the tactic clearly was effective. This Wednesday-night crowd rivaled that of Saturday's. Shelby was not mentioned by name, but the street crowd had come to expect her when the popular Collins scheduled a drop-in like this. Shelby doesn't mind. It is a compliment, and she knows it. She is always the "special guest" hinted to in casual announcements such as this.

The patron cluster of a dozen has grown to a near-capacity crowd of seventy-five as the musical pair takes stage. Shelby feels a familiar and always welcome stirring, remembering her earliest solo performances upon her fresh arrival to the city of music. "Dreamer" was the breakthrough, autobiographical for her, perhaps others. Corb's endorsement of the naive and talented singer's first release was certainly beneficial. Her fans associate the mantra with her, and she with the song. Calmness is returning; anxiety is just a speck of dirt on the newly polished floors of the Country Chord.

The new proprietor, Sam—a transplanted Rhode Islander—handles a gracious introduction for the nine-o'clock session. He looks relieved with the largest turnout since the club was refurbished. Corb has drawn in a nice, and hopefully nicely paying, crowd for the indebted new owner. Sam's smile is genuine. He's invested nearly a quarter of a million in this startup, and he needs the success.

Corb leads the way. She and he are smooth and effective musical partners as they alternate songs and even swap one with each other. She, as a local but lesser-known songwriter, plays "Swampy and Dirty," one of Corb's chart climbers. Corb returns the gesture by performing "Fresh Flowers," astutely exchanging a few *she*s for a highly personal *I*, first person. Corb is always adept at selling a song, including the minor adjustments needed to please his audience to respond to the musical situation. The consummate performer he is, always.

Following a break, the singers sprinkle tidbits of musical songwriting tips, humorous and also encouraging lessons that are absorbed by the budding musicians sitting in the crowd. Tourists and local folks dropping in enjoy the musings as well. Patrons are smiling, well liquored, though some are distracted away from the talented duo.

Shelby nears the end of the song list by announcing the release of her newest single, "Bad Dreams." With an aggressive coupling of guitar, attitude, and energy, the song bursts out to the audience.

> Is there truth to the rumor you're playing the field?
> Same story repeated. More lies are revealed.
> To think that you loved me could calm all my fears.
> But all that you gave me were oceans of tears.

The audience is taken aback by the radical departure from her feel-good songs, but the in-your-face lyrics and raw guitar licks stir up the crowd. Shelby bangs out the closing lines as Corb claps his hands rhythmically overhead. Slowing down and pausing with her guitar, the entertainer closes the song with a raspy voice—uttering but not singing the closure:

> You've got your nightmares, and I've got one too
> The nightmare of lying, believing it's you
> It's waking beside me. I've fought it for years.
> The thought that I love you?

The song reaches a close, with Shelby's spoken ending absorbed with eagerness by those who are attentive—"You figure out if it's true."

The musical story awakens a dormant pain inside a few of the ladies. "Do it, girl" and "Hell yeahs" are echoed and bounced inside the bar. Even guys in love elbow their girlfriends with good-natured approval at two or three of the round tables. Shelby rolls into the show's end by announcing the release of her newest single, "Bygone, By Golly," which was expected to debut in the top twenty on the country charts. Groundbreaking for her in terms of lyrics and genre-bending, it was predicted to arrive high in the pop charts as well.

Corb smiles as she plays the encore. Tables of guests stir in their chairs, some heading to the restroom, others for a smoke. Barker stirs up a handful of people with a rhythmic boot tap. His entourage replicates the move as the Hess fan club energizes.

∞

Shelby can't decide which to respond to first: the buzzing of her cell phone or the knock on her front door. The pounding grows louder as she hears Barker's heady voice calling her name, "Shelby. Shel. Open the freakin' door!" She clutches the cell, heading to greet Barker and glances at the caller ID within her hand. Corb.

The hefty engineer nearly forces his way into the door. "Check your news app. Call up local. You need to hear this."

Corb's number flashes up again, the buzzing repeating its six hums before she selects the Nashville news–

application logo. Her stomach tenses up. Her hands begin to shake as the chill of the news appears on her handheld phone. As always, the phone flashes up the local weather in bold numbers. Today's current temp is an unseasonably cold thirty-two. Black ice is expected on secondary roads. Chillier than normal. Barker squeezes her hand, startling her. She presses the news icon, expecting to see her name and the newly recorded song title on a hits chart. Instead, she is hammered by a bright red headline of the Web-based news channel.

Teenage girl found dead in abandoned cinema.

Her eyes scroll up to meet Barker's. Corb rings again.

Corb's voice carries with it another false positive, a serious coolness that reflects concern, yet perhaps a rehearsed slowness to hold Shelby's nerves steady as he asks her if she knows. She responds to her friend's queries of "How're you doing?" "Did you read the article?" and "Have the sheriff's department deputies contacted you yet?" Her words are echoes, more like incoherent sounds and spontaneous utterances as she ends the call with Corb. She thinks she said something about calling him back; she isn't sure. Trembling, her fingers hit the screen again, scrolling down the miniature font until she turns the phone crossways for a better view. The screen is larger; the text of the story even more so.

Shelby reads on.

"Sumner County deputies responded to a 911 call just before three this morning at the former Regalia Cinema, located at 34550 West Veterans Highway on a report of a body found by a security guard. The guard discovered a body—a young woman, perhaps a teenager—in the abandoned theater. The female had apparently taken her own life by hanging. The investigation continues as the Sheriff's Department cordoned off the cinema to complete its investigation. The body has not been identified."

Amen icy cinema. Amen icy cinema.

"Shelby. I'm tellin' you. It's backmasking. There's something evil here. I tried to tell you. Do you think this is just a coincidence now? Cinema? Icy? The building was abandoned, you know. Freezing inside. And it's freezing outside." The engineer senses his words being absorbed by the young stunned singer.

Her thoughts are a blur. Amen icy cinema, amen icy cinema. Evil. A sin is alive.

Bad dreams on a day like this. Bad dreams on a day like this.

The distraught country singer is confused. Vaguely remembering the balance of the conversation, she sits on her couch, eventually succumbing to a stoic trance. Barker had left. Hours clicked off without her awareness. Was it sleep or a loss of consciousness? She isn't sure. Shelby will call Corb once her mind clears up a bit. Corb will calm her, assure her, and give her some sense of direction.

∞

An intensive interrogation, much more so than the first: questions, verbal prodding, the intrusive camera along with suspicions, and innuendos. Shelby is no longer safe in responding to the detective's inquiries. She'd revealed everything to Corb she could think of when she returned his call that dreadful Thursday. After hours of talking, both on the call and at his home, Shelby called for reinforcements and protection. She lawyered up on her return to the Sumner County station. Completely innocent, she no longer has confidence that the process will be objective or fair. Regardless, she wants the strength and advisement of legal counsel to support her, knowing the zealousness of rising law-enforcement stars on the Sheriff's staff. Aggressive egos get the unstable surge to break the case with her in the middle as a person of interest—or perhaps more. Her capable lawyer, Kirk Sebastian, tutored her that there is no good-cop-bad-cop scenario. She is to presume the worst.

Contrary to what some entertainment gurus think, notoriety and headlines do not always sell records or boost downloads. "Bad Dreams" is immediately banned from airplay. Shelby has no agent, but at the advice of Corb and Sebastian, they decide to not protest the banishment from the muscled radio networks and Web sites. Sales tanked. Her sales volume of "Sideways" dried up immediately after eighty thousand downloads. The shelving of "Bad Dreams" parked sales at a paltry three thousand as the news hit. Disturbing was the revelation that she allegedly—and intentionally—had incorporated satanic messages within her work. Sebastian, aggressively using the media as it suited Shelby's cause, vehemently pushed back at the biased sheriff's team as to how the rumor leaked out about the notes and backmasking.

The growing tsunami of blackness, an overwhelming wave of guilt, washes over Shelby. *Guilt from what?* she questions. She hadn't done anything, yet the body count of teenage girls is at two, perhaps more as revelations occur. Perception is growing that she is complicit in the process. The mainstream media, unfettered but for the pushback from the lawyer, stops short of actual accusations due to fear of litigation. Liberal online streamers, who customarily were advocates for the entertainment industry, scoff at the thought that she is blameless. Her local clique of artists is mixed within their ranges of believability on the likelihood of her involvement.

Phonetic reversal, whether intentional through the recording process or inadvertent in the final mixes, could not have occurred without someone—Barker, perhaps—being a player. Barker Smythe's thirty-year reputation is impeccable, in spite of his fascination with backmasking. Thus, there is filtered encouragement but not all-out support for the image-battered Shelby Hess. Most musical counterparts, producers, and technicians she's met in her tenure in Nashville keep a safe distance. Shelby perceives she is viewed as flawed at the least, snakebit at worst. The venom will stream into their blood if they get too close.

Barker had certainly stepped back. Her curtness toward him repeated itself after his revelation of the first backward message. Shelby struggles with the cause of her coldness toward him. Is she hesitant to absorb the horrid truth of the sinister messages? Does she resent the concept that he may be on to something? More likely, she ventures to think it is his self-promoting obsession that he is point-point accurate: backmasking is not random but created and propagated by some being or specimen. Human or not, it matters little to Barker.

Shelby didn't commit to any additional recording sessions, her emotions drained and her mind jumbled. Her life is a mud pit with no bottom, thrown into it by the impact of the deaths and messages. No longer burdened by the lives of the two deceased teenagers, the former singer is on hiatus. She is craving any nourishment for life, any ray of hope that this will soon end. Yet she knows gut deep, it can end, but won't.

Her mind is no longer capable of processing or pondering the jagged events. Faces blur from the near and faraway past: fans, critics, shallow friends, and the University of Tennessee–shirt-wearing antagonist. Did she really see him? Did Elle approach her after a concert, and did Shelby, in her carelessness, fail to warmly greet the young eager fan? What about Leslie Pankton, the second young girl? Was she an ignored fan also? A stalker?

Shelby's fragile family ties, translucent and dormant since her departure from Seattle, are not strengthened by the crisis. Her mother, Mary Ellen, called a few times as the news of the twisted suicides and the cursed musical messages reached national proportions. The distraught singer did make an effort at restoring the severed ties, fingering her tattoo as she talked at length with her still-single parent. Shelby rubs the neck art, cringing that just as the artistic expression cannot be removed, neither can the wounds of this trauma. "What's next?" she'd blurt out in tears. Mary Ellen's words are commendable but ineffective. The distance is more than geographic. Shelby insists that her mom not make the trip from her former hometown to here. There's too much risk, she conveys to the well-meaning parent, of something happening. Shelby remembers using the words *insanity*, perhaps *demonic*. In reality, Shelby knows that this woman is not equipped in any way to be a healing influence within this death horror.

Corb stands by her, strong and determined. Assured that he has no role in the evaporation of this trauma, he continues his gigs and links up with her near daily. When she was in a medically induced sleep, his calls became recorded devotions that she'd replay again and again to get her through the day—sometimes through the hour. Corb's expressions are frequently a compassionate salve, helping as she endures hours of questioning by detectives, agents, and others in the law-enforcement hierarchy. A prominent headline-screaming story now, she trusts no one but Corb. Her attorney she relies on but doesn't fully commit to him personally. Sebastian plays his role quite well; she stays in his persistent shadow constantly.

∞

Corb Collin's "More Love" tour is viewed favorably, drawing in throngs of up to ten thousand at state fairs, major festivals, and stand-alone venues. Sales are climbing steadily, and Shelby's role as opening act is parked, replaced by Mandy. The hyphen-named singer leaves zero emotional support for Shelby. With Ms. Clifford-Parson, business is business, Shelby is forced to conclude. Corb is held unaccountable for the plight of the dead girls in spite of his continuing to play Shelby's creations. Mandy still compliments Corb well. While aggressive and arrogant, she glows from incredible live-audience energy with a powerful voice to match. Crowds at the local events stroll around the bleacher seating and stand in line for hours to catch a spot at the state-sponsored concert. Scalpers outside of the pair's concerts are pleased with the prosperity of their curbside ticket sales.

The exposure and energy soon rocket Corb Collins to the top slot on popular download sites; Mandy Clifford-Parsons is just behind. Shelby Hess is merely a shadow of reality, like an erased pencil mark on a lyric sheet. Her image as once promising and likeable is decimated by a scathing piece in the monthly Web-based newsletter *Nashville Rises*. The industry publication, with a propensity to allow editorial politics to taint its news of the regional music scene, is merciless in lambasting Shelby. While those from the area may rhetorically ask, "How could she not know?" or reflect that this was more than a coincidence, *Rises* editor Jon Rittaglio inks it more bluntly: "Shelby Hess wrote the messages. Sold it. And pulled the trigger and held the rope. The deaths of these innocent girls are on Hess."

Attorney Sebastian immediately spurted out well-seasoned and articulate rebuttals, but the bomb was dropped. Shelby is now the person of focus for guilt by media, being dragged toward emotional and spiritual suicide herself, as well as perhaps a criminal prosecution in the coming months.

∞

Scraping some grit from his filthy cuticles, Bobby Ray Jenson returns to his obsession. He deems the phonetic-reversed lyrics of Shelby Hess as prophetic messages. His craving is the underbelly of music. Bobby Ray is an explorer, a spelunker into the cavernous guts of songs. Formerly an information technician with an automaker, he's been unincorporated now for seven years, scrounging his way through two-weeks late rent and skimpy meals through government handouts, church weaknesses, and theft. In his below-street-grade apartment, rare in the flat-slab construction of the newer parts of the spread-out city, he hovers over renegade studio equipment and computer paraphernalia. Bobby Ray views himself as a pioneer, a hero to the eternal forces of good and evil. A masked man, he calls himself, or perhaps a back masked man. With a mission to uncover each hidden musical message, Bobby Ray is impassioned toward gold mining for evil messages. Phonetic reversal is his calling; the revelation and distribution of each message, his mantra.

His scarred end table is littered with dozens of scribbled notes. Most are incomplete sentences or incoherent phrases culled from hours of listening to musical compositions from Tennesseans and other musical migrants. He'd heard of the rock bands' reverse messages from an earlier era. Wary at first, he became immersed in the sector of artistry that had lain dormant for decades. A smattering of others were primarily keyed to rock music and heavy metal. Bobby Ray considers himself the lone pursuer of backmasking within the country world. Not objective, he admits to himself, he often force-feeds his thoughts into each lyrical secret, drawing conclusions that may be a stretch to most listeners. His response—to himself no less, as no such conversations occurred with musical fans—is that he has a gift, a divine bestowing that allows him to hear thoughts that others don't. His inventory of threats, prophecies, and proclamations is growing by the month.

The madman's exposure of Shelby Hess was deliberate. "The foolish whore," he curses. She'd slept her way to musical fame with Corb Collins, he concluded. *Who knows who else she screwed, man or woman?* Poring over her songs, he collected and listened to thirteen of her creations. While working as a janitorial night laborer at Best Track Studio, he retrieved four scratched-up lyric sheets authored by the contemptible slut Hess. Matching the lyric sheet to eventual production releases, he burned a compact disc and loaded them into his stolen laptop at the dingy apartment. Within a few sessions, some of which were twelve hours straight in duration, Bobby Ray is convinced he has uncovered the sick messages of her music. Played backwards—an easy task when he applies his still-sharp analytical right-brain hemisphere—Bobby Ray exploded with excitement when the first message came out of the musical womb.

Evil a sin is alive. Clearly conveyed in one of Shelby's earliest hits, the words both excite and motivate the technical genius. Death reeks from each word. He absorbs the message as if he not only wrote it but is assigned to its fulfillment. His choice of execution is to simply, but in a clandestine manner, be the messenger. The harbinger of death is to be delivered by him, but to whom? He relies on meditation, fueled by obsession, concluding that he will know who, when, and where in good time. After all, he is destined to be infamous for his deeds, yet he also wants to enjoy the perversion—the suffering brought on by his excavations and conveyance of twisted musical lyrics.

Nashville is like Hollywood with a guitar, filled with thousands of starstruck girls, many of whom arrived in a battered car with an even more battered guitar and foolish dreams of making it on the charts. Some—like Hess, he presumes—used every possible tactic to make it big, though foolishly, and the bulk of them crawl back home, penniless, broken, and exhausted. Bobby Ray knows the city well and is a frequent visitor to the clubs and singer hangouts. Adept at picking out weak and struggling singers, he preys on those who are susceptible to his hollow compliments, to his intuitive ability to get inside their pretty little heads. Guy or gal, it makes no difference to him.

He befriended several performers, those who had been invited to open-mike nights or amateur contests throughout the city. Three of the players became his disciples, of sorts. He's scrubbed himself presentable, weaning each from the influence of families back home or their respective local counterparts. Capturing them after a performance, Bobby Ray both seduces and encompasses them with a shroud of false sincerity.

One singer remained somewhat aloof: a young man barely eighteen, from Columbus, Ohio, he recalls. Timothy Ledger. Ledger left Bobby Ray about three or so months ago. He never was heard from since. Bobby Ray had hoped this skinny guy would be his first back masked prophecy, but he never knew for sure. Ledger had a handwritten note from the B-Ray courier pressed into his palm following a three-song set in October. The message was lifted from one of Shelby Hess's songs. Bobby Ray had expected to flip open a crumpled newspaper from the local Panera and see the headline, "Young Singer Found Dead. Foul Play Suspected; Shelby Hess Implicated."

No news story broke out. Not for several months, nearly a year to be exact. And not after his copious grooming of the other two musical puppets. Like a growing cancer, his messages extracted from Hess's music are forced into each remaining singer's brains, expanding until each has no ability to rationally think on their own.

Elle comes first and is the easiest. With crappy songs and mediocre string ability, she is not only a simple target but a simpleton as well. She tells him that she hails from Jackson, Mississippi, the adopted daughter of a former itinerant pastor who'd struggled with self-esteem while in school, finally dropping out for a midnight escape to Tennessee. Bobby Ray smothers Elle, she with her desperate loneliness, offering her hand-scribed notes with an upbeat tone to them. He then manipulates her by slowly tweaking the letters, using a subtle degree of cynicism within the notes, and a sinister seed is planted in her mind. Elle is gullible, almost stupid. Like heat turned up slowly on a stovetop pan of water, the temperature rises until the night that she is given the ominous "evil is alive" note.

The news excites him. It arouses his psyche, and Elle could not have played it out better. Perhaps she was seeking redemption, a spiritual return to her adoptive parent's upbringing. The young girl's pew discovery and bloody death is first thought a tragic suicide. It was only later that her demise rekindled media interest. Just as Shelby Hess's songs had to be played backward to hear an alternate message, the second singer's death, a Leslie Pankton, had to be played backward, back to Elle's, to appreciate the sequence. Astute observers are now seeing the connection with phonetic reversal. "Play the deaths back," mumbles Bobby Ray. "Play them back to get to the music."

The cinema suicide is not planned by Bobby Ray. Killing is not his forte. He pathetically, and without any emotion, leaves the method of termination up to the participants, to the failed guitar player and failed artists like Pankton. *This is a masterful maneuver*, he muses. The cold empty theater, unheated and rarely bothered by internal security guards or by outside roaming police patrols, stands as a welcoming cavern for a distressed singer who soon reaches the end of her rope. Bobby Ray finds this death act invigorating and intricately perfect. Leslie absorbs his backward—now unmasked—message and is the star and sole performer in her end-of-life hanging. Bobby Ray deems her a bit shrewder than Elle. The selection of the building and the choice of her method of death require considerably more thought than the first act. Elle's suicide was an act of desperation; Leslie's, an act of obedience.

The messenger is pleased by desperation. Obedience thrills him.

∞

Shelby stretches awake from another nightmare, this one ongoing in her consciousness since Elle's death and pounded harder by the hanging by Leslie. The tired replay of the two deaths wears her into interim sleep. The story line plays over and over again whether she is awake or prone in her satin-covered bed. Glancing down at the nightstand, she views three bottles of temporary reprieve from depression, legitimate appetizers from her psychiatrist. Once a healthy and capable jogger and artist, she barely recognizes the haggard-looking woman in the morning mirrors.

Six months since her last performance at the Chord, Shelby views her guitar sitting isolated in the corner of the bedroom. Dust is already graying its high-gloss finish. Scattered on the floor are handwritten lyric sheets, mostly unfinished, discarded like used tissues. Still wearing smelly flannel pajama bottoms and a once-white tank top, she ventures out of the living room feeling like she hasn't showered in days. Perhaps not. Her dry eyes glance at the clock, reading 11:42 a.m., with sunlight filtering onto a vase of depleted roses, drooped and sad-looking.

The former singer and renowned opening act steps to the door of her condo, hoping some fresh air will wash into her lungs. In another time, she could suck in a deep breath and feel the energy flow down into her toes. Twisting the knob, she swings the chocolate-brown door back and randomly stares at the parking lot, smattered with a few cars. Walkers are absent as they work at their professions indoors, as she once had. The air is pleasant but not helpful. The carefully landscaped and pruned shrubs are seasonally colorful but otherwise unremarkable. She no longer is aware that chords to be played are hanging from each leaf. Lyrics to be scribbled down are sleeping within each blossom, waiting to be lifted out.

Shelby's attention is drawn to the front step. Drab concrete with broom streaks is dotted by a crumpled piece of paper. About half a page, folded over with faint grays of finger smudges on the crease line. Stooping down and nearly losing her balance from the atrophy of her leg muscles over time, she lifts the paper to reading level. Reversing the fold, her eyes stop at a snapshot of the penned words.

Pilz me pilz me lay doun

The door keeps its open greeting, offering her a welcome back. Dizzy, she balances herself with the threshold and reenters the unswept living room. Her gait becomes a stagger as she weaves her way back to the bedroom. Shelby lifts each bottle from the tabletop, shaking the silent air within them as the pills respond with a rattle. She feels just one emotion: remorse at not gulping them down sooner.

Pilz me pilz me lay doun

Splashing her face with cold water, she gulps down the remaining caplets with a handful of water from the faucet, gagging on the mass. Legitimate appetizers had become a one-course entrée. The medicated girl drops the note, drops her arms, and collapses onto the cold tiled floor.

∞

Omar Remis, physician, scribbles a few notes on his clipboard and directs the nurse to enter text into the computer touch-screen pad anchored in the patient's room. Nodding, he graciously unclicks his pen and secures the notepad under his left arm.

"Thanks, Sarah. I know you've pulled a double shift, but I'm sure our young star appreciates you checking on her so late in the day." Turning on his athletic shoes, the psychiatrist exits the room.

Sarah Brighton, RN, fingers the clear IV tube and, sensing moistness, checks a fitting for tightness. She twists the fitting ever so slightly and, satisfied that the leak is cured, enters another notation into the patient record. The nurse, employed at the mental-health wing of Nashville's Sacred Heart Hospital since last December, was once an aspiring singer. She and her beau, now-husband Craig, circuited Nashville's Music Row for nearly four years. Sarah spun off briefly on her own, but Craig's romantic Memorial Day proposal softly led her heart in another direction. And into another life: caring for others.

Completing her nursing degree at Vanderbilt, Sarah had no time to perform at the Blue Bird, the Country Chord, or her other favorites. The marriage to Craig was joyous, coming upon her graduation and just after she completed her licensing exam. Her songs are now warm relics, stored quietly and unanimated in her laptop back home. The once-used Gibson guitar keeps its place in the back of the spare bedroom closet, its dusty case an ignored reminder of dreams that once were.

Glancing down at the frail figure in the bed, the nurse aches with compassion for what once was and for songs unwritten. She gently strokes the auburn tresses of Shelby Hess, matted and stringy from months of medicated rest in the well-funded hospital wing. A registered nurse by trade, Sarah is a devoted fan by commitment. Embarrassed to openly share her admiration for the fallen singer, she instead offers comforting words to a motionless body, gently caressing the fingers that proudly pressed chords and strummed rhythms. Her devotion to Shelby is not rewarded with any marked improvement nor a response. Dr. Remis is empathetic to her dilemma: that of hurting so much for the former rising star to recover and simultaneously striving to be a caring health provider with equal treatment to each of the patients on her shift.

Sarah dares not linger, though she touches the right hand of the guitar player, pondering the memories of watching Shelby perform once with Corb at the Country Chord. The fall was tragic. The death count ended at just two, fortunately. Sarah doesn't remember the names of those who took their own lives, nor that of the itinerant stalker who apparently had seduced each musician into his sick world of psychological manipulation. The stalker was a coward who slashed himself and bled to death hours before his expected arrest in the case involving the once-apparent but now-questionable suicides.

The media suggested—some more than others—that Shelby was an active participant in the string of events until the beleaguered artist succumbed to prescription-drug addiction. Empathy now replaced skepticism. Love returned, but not her career, as Shelby Hess transitioned from fallen star to drug addict to ward of the court, ordered into a lengthy full-time stay at Sacred Heart. Sarah, misty-eyed, wishes healing for Shelby, author of hits that filled the nurse's ears near daily for several years. She memorized the lyrics of smashes such as "Sideways," "Quick Forever," "City Girls and Country Curls"—even "Bad Dreams"—rejecting as unbelievable the notion that backmasking lay hidden among the chords, among the words authored by Shelby.

The RN completes her tasks, knowing that she will never complete her role as adoring fan of the wonderful Shelby Hess. Gathering her thoughts and checking that her stethoscope is in place, Sarah air-fingers a few chords from today's selected Shelby song and leaves the private room. Shelby rests, still.

With her watch reading near noon, Sarah hits the first-floor elevator button and drops down to the visitor lobby. Stepping out of the elevator, she smiles both out of respect and admiration. The chair is warmed as always on Sunday mornings by the tanned image of a country superstar. His leather boots are familiar, his jeans the familiar faded black. He mindlessly flips through a sporting news magazine, three months old and unlabeled, pulling the imagined wrinkles out of his white T-shirt. Sarah sees his gray cap, labeled with the highly recognized double-C letters embroidered upon a silk-screened electric guitar logo, lying on the floor next to him.

Sarah pauses for a moment, observing the quiet strength of the talented performer, and reflects on his commitment that is as defined as hers. Reaching toward the visitor, the committed psychiatric nurse offers a handshake to the legend.

Without hesitation, he stands and returns the gesture, pulling the nurse gently to him as the pair of devoted fans share an embrace that is warming, respectful, and precise.

Sarah steps back and holds his hands gently then releases. The singer's status never impacts his sincerity. He and Sarah are comfortable with themselves and their shared commitment toward Shelby. Sarah fingers her wedding band, grateful for Craig, and sees an untanned line on the left ring finger of her friend as he retrieves his cap.

"You can go in now," Sarah instructs softly, wiping her eyes with the back of her hand.

"Thanks, Sarah. We're always hopeful, aren't we?" With those words—uttered at each visit since Sarah can recall—Corb Collins tips his cap to her. Turning on his heels, Corb heads toward the elevator to seek out his number-one fan. She was just another dreamer once, just like him.

Class of Twenty-Seven

The deep bass ringtone echoes through the foyer. The sound mimics a heavy rock guitar, fitting since the owner of the mansion is rock legend Robert James "BJ" McClelland. The tone is a musical burp: high, low, high. Each note is both familiar and a bit humorous to me. I'd arrived just moments ago, stepping inside to absorb the massive home. Flattered that BJ invited me to the event, I'm awed at the six-foot-wide clef note embossed on the floor, inlaid with handcrafted wood. The image is just short of gaudy.

The door chime rings again, breaking BJ from his efforts in welcoming me.

Her voice isn't any more familiar than her face to me as BJ opens the front door. She stands on the chipped marble front step, arms wide as if her newly seen host is a holiday gift to be unwrapped.

"Robert James, love. I've missed you so." A chestnut-haired woman with the densest red lip color I'd ever seen reaches and pulls BJ into an embrace. She closes her eyes, escaping into a recollection that is more than friendly. "What's it been, five years again?"

BJ shares in the affection of her embrace, not sensing my slight hint of embarrassment or my awkward staring. Hesitant to cool this quasi-intimate moment, I put my rehearsed greeting in park. I defer to BJ, the host. Looking away, I take in the musical artwork again and dart my eyes sideways to burgundy-colored drapes that are dust-covered.

"Linda, babe, you're still looking good." There's a twinge of innuendo in BJ's response. The emphasis is equally emphatic on both words *still* and *good*. I smile, BJ notices, Linda beams. She's graceful, magical. "The timing is perfect, Linda. You always know how to make an entrance. Sexy's what it is. Plain sexy." Linda curls her arm around BJ, tossing her hair. She gives me a smile that melts my ego to knee level.

"Hello. Have we met? I'm Linda. Linda Bolero." She warmly extends her jeweled hand toward me. It rests on my arm as softly as a butterfly.

BJ curses apologetically, asking for a reprieve from his clumsy manners, crude as they may be. "Sorry, man. My head must be up somewhere dark. But it's been a few years since I threw a party. Sorry. Dexter, meet Linda. Linda, this is Dexter Davis."

"Linda? The Linda Bolero? My grandfather grew up listening to your—"

Crap, I murmur, wishing I could have a vocal vacuum and suck the words back into my mouth. Though my blurting is factual, I hated the reference to her era. My Grandpa Charlie drove his first-date car and slurped his first French kiss to The Bolero's classic hit, "Hold Me Like You Mean It." The smash topped the charts his final year in school as a junior before he dropped out to work the farm. "Sultry. Sultry's what the song was," Grandpa had said. *Still is*, I muse. *Still is*.

The Bolero lead singer snaps me back to the moment and to her aura. "Please, it's fine. It was eons ago. And as they say, good music is timeless."

"What I mean is, yeah, well 'Hold Me' is forever. It's still the song in my head in the morning more times than I count. I love that song!" Damage limited, I hope. Minimized more so by Linda's graciousness than by my feeble effort to smooth my verbal stumble. Star struck, I am.

"Dex is a rookie with us. First timer," BJ interjects, helping to take the redness away from my face. "Did you hear about the Honeysuckles? They came out of Pinebluff two or three years ago."

"You're a member of the Honeysuckles? Did you sing lead?" Linda's query is kind, uninformed.

"I founded the group. We mimicked Three Dog Night's model, having three of us split lead vocals on most songs. Musically, it worked and kept the egos in harmony." *TMI*, I think. I'm in the rock music foyer of the celebrated BJ

McClelland and smiling with Linda Bolero. *Take it slowly, Dexter. Slowly.*

"I was so influenced by your work, Ms. Bolero. Linda." Past tense? I *still* am. I pause for effect. "You rolled out hit after hit. 'Last Chance,' 'Baby's Getting It,' 'Time Will Tell.' Love them all."

"Three Grammy nods and a half dozen top tens." BJ's eyes sparkle at his memorized news flash. "Wasn't 'Hold Me' in '58, the first year they were awarded?" He pauses for effect and, with a mischievous gleam in his eyes, looks suggestively at Linda. "Hold Me."

"I never forget the magic words." With this retort, Linda places her scented palms on BJ's bearded cheeks and, as if on cue, wetly kisses him full mouth. She eases back with a trademarked Bolero smile. "By the way, the Grammys started the year after Sinatra's peak. That sure boosted my chances."

What am I missing between these two? The blatant display of affection seems a bit but much here in the foyer. I search for a tidbit to bring me into the picture. Somewhere there's a clue, maybe a rite of passage here. My pulse jumps at the fantasy of a kiss by—*with*—Linda Bolero.

BJ licks his lips to taste the crooner's kiss. "Three ceremonies and fifteen years. You're amazing, Linda." I push my hands into my jeans pockets, realizing that I want to keep them safe and away from Linda. Not a natural hugger, I don't trust myself to reach out and express my attraction to her.

"Let's join the others." BJ resumes his host role and leads us back to the living room. Linda seems to know the way, stepping ahead of BJ. Her move is intentional, anticipatory. She's been here before and reflects an eagerness to see others.

"Don't mind the jerks, Dexter." BJ's admonition comes as a start. "All the dudes here received an invitation, though not all arrived here by choice. We each have a story to tell. Music kinda takes a backseat at these reunions."

I notice his sweat-dampened satin shirt: an ivory-silver with billowing sleeves. Definitely seventies, along with his tightly curled mane of hair now smattered with white. McClelland, the typical rock star. He's crusty yet friendly with a drained talent bucket that is now as rusty as his voice. He'd not been on my list of favorites. The Brash, a heavy metal group born in New York City, had drugged, plugged, and forced its way to the top of the rock music world. BJ was its charismatic lead singer and acidhead. The group imploded somewhere between the Nixon Watergate scandal and voting out of Jimmy Carter. Now, an eternity later, the rocker's chocolate-leather pants were put on wet and dried to a near-obscene tightness. His face is gaunt; his eyes are foggy but still focused.

I never knew if he kicked his addictions or not. And there were many demons.

I'd entered the expansive chamber as a social and musical counterpart of both BJ McClelland and Linda Bolero. He, the screaming singer who drew crowds by the thousands; she, the crooner-turned actress; and me, the harmonizing balladeer from the deep Southwest. I'd only appeared in a few larger venues, always a lower card at the larger festivals of summer. My one kudo nomination came three years before the Grammy categories—and total number of awards—were sliced by half. My award—our Honeysuckle *shared* award—for best Americana album for 2011 is merely an asterisk.

"BJ, who's your new sidekick? You decide to go folksy on me?"

BJ flips him the bird. The Brash front man's smile is split between friendly familiarity and contempt. "Go to hell, Stanton."

"Been there, done that." Stanton reacts. "Trapper. Trapper Stanton."

The burly entertainer looks larger than life, standing some six inches taller than my six-foot frame. His muscular hand grasps mine with an intentional but not injury-inducing squeeze. Trapper displays his uniform: a red and black plaid shirt, sans sleeves; cream-colored cowboy hat with sweat stains and fingerprints just below the brim (and more than likely on top as well). Well-washed black jeans sport small blotches of gray and are lopped over the top of snakeskin boots. Real snakeskin, not fake, I conclude.

His exaggerated belt buckle is smoky-gray pewter with an embossed American flag. I draw my eyes away so as not to stare at his midsection. I think the buckle reads "God Bless Vets."

"Dexter Davis, Honeysuckles." I offer. The clue is intended to avoid another age-based comment as I did with Linda. *Give him a clue*, I think. *He has no idea who I am.*

"'Up and Ready'? Wasn't that the name of your disc back a few years? Had it. Loved it!"

Really? I think. Trapper Stanton, the biggest—in both size and image—country music star in the past decade knows *my* work? I'm leery, but he'd done his prep work. Sign of a great entertainer. Know when and where to flatter your audience. But again, though I never felt comfortable accepting BJ's invitation, I deserve to be here. I qualified.

"Thanks, Mr. Stanton. I've been a huge fan of yours. I'm flattered that you've heard my music." *Nice*, Dexter. *Play it modest*. This guy sold one-point-two and hit platinum his first year alone. Gold is for amateurs. Our initial CD, 'Up and Ready,' was gold, and that only meant half a million in sales. Trapper was double platinum several years running.

"Crunchin' country, Mr. Stanton, is what I call it. Rough, good, and powerful crunchin' country." Hopefully, my intimidation is hidden but not my admiration.

"Good choice of words. And I'm just Trapper to everyone. Started out as Tommy. Trapper had a ring to it."

His sleeves have a masculine strength to them, as do the scars marking his forearms. The image of his now-damaged arm is not repugnant, but it is alarming. The etchings on his forearms are mix of tainted purple burn marks and healed incisions that vein up and down as if made by a drunken tattoo artist. His cheeks look scuffed, as if he had shaved with a steel wool pad. The story of the crash was spewed nationally within an instant. Homemade videos, some distasteful, showing the burning wreckage, were in millions of mobile phone boxes moments after Trapper's classic car caromed off Tennessee's Highway 44. The rare Jaguar convertible was original to the core, with no airbags or safety belts, leaving Trapper unprotected. The singer, though sober, was projected onto the dry, rolling landscape. The fiery crash shattered the calmness of the wooded countryside.

Following Linda, BJ, Trapper, and I saunter through the aged-stained hallway. We pass by a partially opened pocket door that shed filtered lamplight into the living room. Peeling flowered wallpaper is the backdrop for dozens of musical monuments and awards. Gold-colored discs of assorted sizes hang in the balance among plaques and other honors. Tributes to artists from various decades, like the bluesy Robert Johnson, hang on the walls.

One string of awards on the back wall is eerie: Malcolm Hale, Brian Jones, Janis Joplin, and Jim Morrison in annual and sequential order. I didn't intend to zero in on the plaques. More so, the display jumped out at me. A Spanky, a Stone, a Pearl and a Door one year after the next; a string of stars who fell like dominos.

I recognize one of the smaller discs as representing my CD, only separated from the others by a darkened font claiming: "'Up and Ready' 2011 Certified 500,000 sold." I'm somewhat embarrassed by its hanging. The modest disc looks childlike next to the traditional extended-play version that is larger, more impressive. Alongside Bolero's three consecutive platinum circles, 'Up and Ready' looks not lonely but isolated. Three million versus my paltry five hundred thousand in sales: Linda is a star; me and the Honeysuckles, simply a speck.

But I'm qualified to be here, I remind myself. Though, *maybe I don't deserve it.* The invitation to the event smells sweet to me, yet bitter.

"Davis!" BJ's voice snaps me back alert. "Stop being so starry-eyed and wake up. Here's someone I'd like you to meet."

The burning blush on my face is apparently noticeable. I see Linda smile politely; Trapper is engrossed in working the flock of musicians and singers like the country-rock politician he is. I spin back toward BJ and pulled there by his knuckled clutch on my inked bicep.

"Dexter, Sandy Giles. You remember Giles from Papillion? Pop trio out of N'Orleans? Sandy's the most famous ex-band member ever to be named to the Hall of Fame. Some sax player'll do anything for a trip to Cleveland. Cleveland, bloody Cleveland." BJ's voice echoes a bit, bouncing around until it lands on nearby ears.

Sandy's hand is on my shoulder before the next blink; his right hand clutches mine in a sincere but weary shake. Bent fingers curl around mine as his eyes reflect a painful grimace.

"Dexter, nice. Hadn't heard much about you, no offense. I'm not in the loop as I was a few years back. BJ colored in the squares for me. First time?"

"First time. Friendly group. I recognize a few people. I'm enjoying it so far," I half-lie.

"It gets better. The first year is the toughest. Denial, coming to this place and having to mix with pricks and saints at the same time." He struggles to inhale, then continues. "It's kind of like the record release parties. Always inviting friends, but the occasional snake crawls in." Sandy's admonition is both accurate and obligatory. "Problem is, attendance each year is mandatory. I never figured that one out."

Mandatory? The word hadn't gotten yet to me. I didn't check my inbox when I left. What would happen if I didn't show?

Glancing about, the group is about twenty now. Others had filtered in as I listened to the idle chatter and the *how-are-yas?* An echo bounces off of the musical memorabilia-covered walls as BJ breaks in with his announcement.

"Ladies and gentlemen, and Trapper." The age-old joke is stale; not so the hors d'oeuvres I long to suck down.

BJ picks up a statuette from an end table near the couch. "It's my pleasure to introduce you to the newest member of our motley crew."

His formality is unnecessary. I and others know what is about to happen, though I only recently imagined going through the actual ceremony here at the mansion.

"The Class of Twenty-Seven was established somewhat by accident." Several attendees chuckle at this; Trapper does not. "I came here over a decade ago. I'd just finished a twelve-city tour with the Brash and did my usual routine with a double groupie and a triple scotch back at the hotel in Brussels. It was my birthday. The tour had pulled in the money and all of Europe was scarfing up our albums. See our platinum over the fireplace? Ours. Mine. I put it there 'cause I run the show."

I'm sure the old rockstar has a direction with this. He meanders, the polite-but-restless team impatiently eggs him—*begs him*—on. He's come to a fork in the road. Now he's going to take it. My amusement at the quote triggers a smile. Outwardly, it works. I look pleased when I need to. *Dexter*, I coach myself, *eyes up.*

"We've been growing as a club, but this is the first time we've added a new member to the Twenty-Sevens for three or four years now. Some of us as musicians caught the wave of stardom by accident. The impeccable timing of a trend with the most opportune good fortune. Others bought their way into the limelight. They had Sugar Daddies, biological or seduced. Some, like me, are just that good," BJ boasts. Guffaws dampen the air with mock aggravation. Trapper rolls his eyes.

Linda nods in her customarily charming way. She's the benefactor of family money, coming from a long line of historical catsup makers. Trapper glares as if he wants to kick the rock runt's aged ass. I peruse the mixture of faces. BJ's review will be mixed.

"I just met Dexter. His is the epitome of the Americana sound, electrified folk with the pulse of country. He's good at it. Worked hard and made it happen. It's a shame to see him give it up so early."

Surprisingly, I feel emotions. Stronger than I expected, though I can't say I was predicting any at all. Still, BJ's insinuation stings a bit. Though he only mentioned how *stardom* was achieved by some, the same could be said of how *membership* was obtained into the Class of Twenty-Seven. The similarities are uncanny: some were sworn in by hard work and persistence, having tried but failed to get in multiple times before succeeding. Trapper didn't really try at all but became eligible at the peak of his fame and of his musical career. Linda's selection came after three decades of consideration. Hers was not so much a lack of qualifications but rather genre. Since when do singers-turned-actresses qualify? Linda stayed true to her personal charm by always being classy. I admit, however, that though her fame as a crooner of finely tuned standards from the forties made her famous; in later years, she turned to film and did quite respectably. But she is here, and I don't mind.

Me? I didn't plan or think about membership. I'd been touring, tired but healthy and feeling indestructible just past my twenty-seventh birthday. The cough started during a gig in Munich, our first of a six-stop tour through Europe. I'd blamed the flu-like symptoms on fatigue and on being road weary. I noticed my soaking of two shirts during a performance. But this was a draining perspiration along with a 105-degree sizzle of a fever. By the third stop, my weight was down seven pounds, and my bass player and drummer had similar symptoms.

My downward health slide was quick, the cause only guessed at by well-trained medical experts. The trip to our next gig in Cardiff, Wales, was a fever-induced blur. Concluding it was the flu, I was poked and stabbed and fed numerous bacteria-fighting meds and injected with IVs. The isolation was the loneliest part. Quarantine is not lonely in itself; it's the lack of freedom to leave that triggers a gut-level anxiety. My stomach was already twisted from the illness. I didn't need the magnified worry of being trapped alone in this Welsh hospital bed.

I do remember the other trip. Sorry, it's not like it really was a *trip*. More like a zip, a whoosh, and a flashing whirl through a peaceful tunnel toward a light. The luminescence at the end of this quick journey still impresses me. The warmth of the light was soothing and continues to linger over my skin. The impetus, whatever or whoever it was, deposited me in front of this mansion. No taxi or anything. Just the whoosh.

So upon reflection, I didn't plan or think about membership. But here I am.

BJ's voice drones away amid my introspection. I snap alert. Am I still smiling?

"And so"—BJ beams—"it is with great pleasure to introduce to you the newest member of the Class of Twenty-Seven: Dexter Davis!"

The cluster of singers claps politely, with body language that reflects sincerity. My face heats up, triggered by a degree of modesty from the attention I'm absorbing. I nod. Linda smiles. Trapper closes in on me with a hard and hearty slap on the back.

"Welcome, Dex!" Trapper's grin matches his country-wide girth. The remnants of his car wreck are still etched into his skin.

Linda remains poised and natural as one who never ages but ends up looking as magnificent as when she first took the stage five decades earlier. A few other seasoned entertainers are more aloof, hesitant in their greetings and acknowledgements. Familiar but nameless faces dot the room. No one else comes forward.

And BJ? He is still as ragged and rough as he was as a nineteen-year-old rocker. Emaciated but highly energetic, he slurs no more now than when his recreational drug use splashed all over his life. He winks a "nice job" toward me. I sense that he has a good heart, just a much-worn one. This is his party and my recognition.

I scan the room, stumbling over what to say. Only a meager thank-you tumbles out of my mouth. Damn nervousness. This verbal stub is not from Linda's stardom like before. It's related more to my twenty-seven-year-old personae and bashful shadow.

Sandy steps over and shakes my hand. "Congrats, my man." I see the nearly healed hole in his throat. The fleshy spot was an air tube opening until the very end. His voice remains caustic, not gravelly in the traditional sense but more like a lumpy computer-generated sound that is easy to understand. *Easy*, I mean in the sense that I pay close attention when Sandy speaks.

I don't dwell on membership. I accept the honor, if you will, of being in the rare company of great singers and musicians who stepped away from the stage. Some, perhaps, were shoved off. Each of us was snatched away years before some had predicted: Trapper, the aggressive country star taken by a flaming car crash; BJ, following one too many needles or snorts; and Sandy, who struggled with throat cancer and was gone more than two years before he hit thirty.

Me? Was it an infected handshake from a well-meaning fan? Tainted food perhaps? Maybe it was some kind of serious and fatal flu. Was my demise accelerated by a soiled needle from a hospital caregiver?

Twenty-seven years old, each of us. Musicians, all.

Time doesn't stand still here at the mansion. In limbo or purgatory or whatever this is, each of us morphs slowly. Each of my now-fellow members seem to have evolved since I last saw their photos. Trapper and Sandy's scars are matured, perhaps fading. Linda's face is etched with age lines that are artistic in their placement and curves. And my fever-reduced weight, if there is such a measurement here, is stable. My jeans no longer need the leather belt.

Membership has its privileges. Keep in mind, membership in the Class of Twenty-Seven isn't the end of the world. It's the beginning of some other beginning's end. Yeah, it's in a song I heard somewhere.

With congratulations and accolades over, each of us mixes and mingles and hobnobs within the rooms of the elegant mansion. Soft music is playing covers of my modest list of hits. I'm flattered but sense that the gesture is to be expected here at the Class of Twenty-Seven's induction party.

The bass guitar-chord sound rings again from the door. BJ, not expecting anyone else, breathes out uneasily.

"I wonder who that could be."

∞

Requiem for the Stars

Robert James "BJ" McClelland, rocker. Born June 24, 1951

"You do what I do and play what I play. You'll get what I get—and deserve it."

Died August 7, 1973 of a self-induced drug overdose, believed to be accidental

∞

Linda Ann Bolero, crooner. Born January 12, 1937

"I never dreamed that I'd ever say I love you, right from the start."

Died September 9, 1964 peacefully in her sleep of an aneurysm

∞

Thomas "Trapper" Stanton, country singer. Born December 12, 1977

"Let's get swampy and dirty."

Died June 1, 2005 in an automobile accident

∞

Sandy Raymond Giles, jazz musician, saxophone. Born April 8, 1958

"Sideways, we enjoy the view. Just me and you."
Died November 29, 1985 of esophageal cancer

∞

Dexter Daniel Davis, Americana singer. Born May 13, 1987
  "I'm just another dreamer in a local band."
  Died August 11, 2014 of an influenza-like virus

∞

Shelby Lynn Hess, country/pop singer. Born March 17, 1987
  "The thought that I love you? You figure out if it's true."
  Died April 9, 2014 of undetermined causes.

Pardon Me

Pardon is such a simple and powerful word—its two-syllable enunciation echoing strength at the beginning followed by a softer, apologetic sound at the end. *Pardon* means something was wrong and now is made whole, like the inadvertent bump of someone in the grocery store. No harm, no foul, and you proceed to the checkout feeling that all is forgiven. At the other extreme is the high power of the word's strength, where a life-changing or life-ending event can't be reversed by a simple apology. *Pardon*, its simplicity secretly competing with its power, often appears out of nowhere in the lives of those who are just as simple and powerful.

The Franklin County Courthouse hovers over a domed foyer, arching to an open conference room. A podium stands in the center at the front of the political theater. The laser-carved Great Seal of the State of Ohio rests ten feet above the podium. The pulpit looks majestic, though a bit travel-weary, as most of the dominant politicians who once stood behind it. Mirroring the sides of the podium, placed back a few feet as if to defer to the next most important speaker to step up to the plate, are two flags. Each rises sleepily from solid-looking poles, one representing the United States of America and a complementary-colored pennant of red, white, and blue representing Ohio. If each patriotic flag had eyes, it would see rows of cushioned chairs that were lined up strategically, eleven wide and eight deep, representing the eighty-eight counties of Ohio.

Most of the seats are filled now, perhaps all but seven or eight. The throng of past and future voters appears no different than a hoard of people anywhere else in the county, or the country for that matter. Hints of sadness rest in the hearts of each person attending—faces mirror the emotion. Flanking on each side of the seating area are aluminum-colored stands with white cardboard placards. Each is marked in deep-blue letters: Victim Advocates and Families Only.

The local network news crews jockey for position, each straightening his or her jacket. One removes a pocket mirror and smiles insincerely into the reflection. Each reporter's look suggests, "I'm ready," but the fatigue in their eyes says, "I look like hell."

In the third chair next to last row sits Cyndi Anne Roberts, widow.

Cyndi has been here for nearly an hour, fidgeting, checking her phone for unattended messages, roaming in and out of the huge government building more than fifteen times since she arrived at 9:03 a.m., the first person to clear security in advance of the news conference. Forty-seven years old, she wears stylish black slacks, coupled with a crisp white blouse that is buttoned to the neck. Her auburn-brown hair is pulled back, revealing small hoop earrings from a Christmas gift of nearly two decades ago. Her northern Ohio navy winter coat rests across her lap. The coat cradles an eight-by-ten color photo of the most handsome man she had ever known, her late husband, Jake.

Jake was not tall but statuesque, like a weight lifter who walked with purpose. His gait was one of strength—confident but never haughty. It was as though there were more muscles that wanted to move than were permitted while he was pedestrian. This photo captures one of her favorite memories, the spontaneous pose of him in his softball uniform displaying the kelly-green script, "Malvern's Place" trimmed in gold and sewn to the light-gray uniform. Ball cap pushed back on his head, he smiled brightly for the snapshot after his three-for-four day and a six-run victory.

Two years younger than her, Jake was the perfect solution to an imperfect world. Bright but not ambitious, kind but not weak, he was the calming switch for her tense inner wiring. Never one to push career above loving, he seemed to flow around her and inside her with placid constancy. Cyndi lifts the photo slightly, pausing to reflect again what he would have looked like now after nineteen-plus years.

No doubt he would have aged graciously, perhaps sporting some gray at the temples, maybe with arms less strong but still capable of pulling her close at the end of a trying day. Cyndi keeps this picture and this picture alone. The image of Jake is clear enough to be understood by the press-conference crowd and large enough to be noticed. She loves him and misses him still.

A sharp blast of air enters the huge building, and its suddenness startles Cyndi from her drift back in time. The echo of footsteps causes the audience to shift and turn in their seats to view the entourage entering the meeting hall. Three uniformed guards lead the way—reservists from what she can tell—in starched-beige fatigues, highly polished black boots, and berets perched to one side. *Quite a show of force*, she muses, though none wear any visible firearms.

The focus of attention is on a silver-haired statesman wearing a classic gray business suit. Governor T. Richard Hambaugh, Democrat, in his sixth and final year of a term-limited tenure, strides aggressively up to the podium and turns to face the audience, looking much older than his sixty-three years. An underweight fledging intern, dressed in pressed khaki slacks, light-blue shirt, and navy blazer, quickly and efficiently clips a wireless microphone to a lapel of the governor's suit coat and then immediately evaporates. The governor moves his eyes robotically from side to side, taking in the panorama of news-media representatives and weary constituents—perhaps some of whom are lawyers, family members, and supportive friends of the victims. The sea of people also includes a salting of his political adversaries who are here, no doubt to gloat over the perceived dastardly decision. News had leaked out, and the much-maligned Hambaugh was obliged to confirm it.

The air of the crowded meeting hall maintains its chill, perhaps from the opened door of minutes earlier or more likely from the gravity of the setting. Cyndi straightens herself in her chair, gently presses her hand upon her husband's photo, and turns her disbelieving attention toward the podium. She has been nearly nauseous for the past week or so, ever since the news tweaked and twittered out about the decision. No, it was the eight decisions by the governor that broke open aging wounds with an emotional blood that was transparent but visible to all around. It is one decision that tore at Cyndi—that made her cry in apprehension again.

The governor lays a stiff sheet of plain white paper onto the podium with hints of finger wrinkles and opaque oily smudges at the top corners. He pushes away the low-keyed murmuring of the attendees with a slap of cold words that both alert and focus each person on him. In clear commanding tones that reflect decisiveness but insincerity, he speaks.

"Ladies and gentlemen, esteemed members of my staff, members of the press, and to each and every citizen of the

Great State of Ohio here today, I thank you for your time and attendance this morning.

"The office of the governor carries with it the needs of twelve million state citizens, including the burden of addressing difficult issues and situations that are challenging at best. I have had the honor and privilege of serving as your governor for the past six years, thanks to your initial and repeated support through the elective process of our great state. The state Constitution empowers me with the responsibility and authority to make decisions that impact some people more than others and to restore to certain people rights and freedoms that were removed by a court system and by decisions reached by juries of peers.

"I am, of course, referring to the power of the pardon. The act of pardoning selected persons means to restore upon them each and every right available as citizens of Ohio. Each of you realize, I am sure, that not only is this power of pardon granted to me exclusively as governor— but has been exercised many times in comparable circumstances by each of my predecessors, Democratic and Republican alike. As I depart the office of the governor and relinquish my role as your leader to the governor-elect, I am simultaneously granting full pardons to eight persons who are either currently incarcerated in our state prison system or who have recently been released to selected supervised assignments."

"Therefore," the governor continues, "I have by proclamation granted full and unencumbered pardons to eight persons as my last formal act of authority as your governor. The pardons are granted to the following…"

Cyndi clicks off the number in her mind, hoping for the eighth name to be read and close out the list before her heart is ripped open. She risks losing her latest meal onto her lap and onto the photographic face of her late beloved Jake. She knows in the recesses of her mind that the dreaded name will be announced, but she had inwardly prayed, begged, cajoled, and hoped for weeks that it will not be. Not after all these years—not after the trauma of the shooting, of the funeral, the bereavement, and long painful years of adjustments to life alone as widow. She already reinvented her entire life. *No, please no! Don't let the name be read.* Cyndi is oblivious to the moans, groans, and curses around her.

"And finally," the governor concludes, "the eighth pardon is granted to Damon Keith Osborne.

Each pardon, which goes into effect one week from today, is made with a careful and copious review of all factors and public records. I took into consideration a wide range of viewpoints and, in some instances, heard directly from family members impacted by the pardons that I was considering. It is clear that these decisions are both difficult to make and controversial to some."

The stirring of the crowd becomes noisy as people shift in their chairs and media members inch closer with the squeaking sounds of athletic shoes and tripods. Breaths of suppressed anger from disturbed family members push out into the empty air of the large room.

The veil of focused deafness to all that was going on around Cyndi immediately disappears. She finds herself in the middle of a vocal thunderstorm of gasps, shouts of "bastard!" and utterances of profanity that rise above the faces of many who sit there in stilted and shocked silence. The governor, in a weak attempt to placate most of the crowd—who are either stunned, angry, or both—pauses to let the announcement absorb into each person. This is a mistake, as he had expected it to be, but he wants to manipulate the record and for the media to reflect that he had shown "considerable patience and empathy with each family member present" in its press release and evening primetime broadcasts.

The governor straightens himself, knowing that he is in no way required to meet with these family members. He felt it somehow politically appropriate to do so. He avoids eye contact with any one person and instead looks beyond the group, concluding his speech with the following stiff statements: "I understand the strong feelings that many of you have with these pardons I have made. While I don't apologize for the decisions, I convey to each of you the deep and thorough thoughts that I had in selecting each person for pardon. Each of these people have been granted the opportunity to begin anew, to start over, to contribute in a meaningful way to society, and to enjoy the rights and privileges available to each of us in the room today. My fellow citizens, I know that you do not agree with these pardons, but I request that you accept them and move forward. Move on."

With this verbal slap, Governor Hambaugh curtly closes the media circus, refusing any and all questions, and removes himself from the podium. The entourage immediately swarms around him, protecting him from the angry and steely eyes of wounded family members, which shoot at him like lasers in the dark. But nothing penetrates the politician's resolve. The honorable governor disappears through an eight-foot-tall walnut door and vanishes.

Move on? Move on? Cyndi's mind echoes, unspoken as her mouth had lost the ability to speak. She feels herself shaking badly from the announcement, her hands quivering as she clutches Jake's picture. Just like that—one governor, one sentence, one decision. And now Damon Keith Osborne, the murderer, walks out the door to live, breathe, and "move on." The years of her appearing in front of the parole board to contest early release wasted. She had, though, missed the last two, as nothing appeared to suggest that Osborne would be considered for a pardon.

She had come alone today and will leave alone, but in a perverse way, Cyndi suddenly feels crowded. She is no longer isolated in the solitude of her time-diluted grief. The thought of Osborne walking free is emotionally inconceivable. He had reportedly been a model prisoner of the Warren Correctional Institute in Lebanon, Ohio, for the sixteen years, three months, and twelve days that he had been locked up in the concrete, steel, and technology-decked human zoo. No doubt he had the benefit of being in a state-run facility, which was overcrowded compared to that of the privately run facilities that were profit-driven and thus craved keeping each resident for as many days as possible. *Yes, that was it*, she thought in a meager attempt to rationalize the release of the murderer: prison overcrowding.

The world had forgotten Jake, forgotten the image of his lifeless body lying on the floor of the convenience store Twenty Plus, its name coming from the twenty or more hours that it remained open each day except Christmas. She had begged Jake to be patient, to wait for another opportunity, or at least better hours. But Jake, lovable as he was, thirsted to work the late evening hours into the early morning as he could hop home for a quick shower after a summer doubleheader and still put in his hours at the store.

It was so senseless. Three pops from the small .22 caliber handgun, and Jake's life was snuffed like a permanent strikeout. According to the coroner's report, Jake was gone immediately. Osborne skirted away with seventy-two dollars. Seventy-two! It barely paid for a tank of gasoline. In a few days, Osborne would be pumping gasoline into his car, perhaps given to him by a loving family member or a feel-gooder immune to the damage that he had caused to Cyndi's life. She ponders if he still remembers seventy-two. Does he remember the three modest slugs, the echo of the gun's sound in the store, his initial denial before the plea bargain?

She had reluctantly agreed to the plea bargain. She was exhausted, had been under outpatient psychiatric care, and could barely summon the energy to keep returning to court as the date of trial drew near. Osborne eventually confessed, expressed remorse, and cooperated with authorities—whatever that means—following the gunning down. Though the prosecutor was willing to go all out and bring Osborne into the weary and time-consuming path of a lifetime conviction and sentence, it was agreed to let the shooter sit for years with his conscience. "Move on," T. Richard said. "Move on!"

∞

As with the senseless killing many years ago, such is the pardon of Osborne, now two years old. I remember it but no longer feel it.

It isn't like it is a healing. Not like it never happened. It is more like reflecting on an old movie seen—but partially forgotten—or a book read three or four times, yet the details have started to fade. Perhaps it's this way with scarring, I think. Nature has a way of assuming control not only of the events that are dropped like bombshells into our lives, but it also has a way of removing the awareness of pain at times when you need it most. It's as though the stories of calamity and crisis are accurate: After the first excruciating pain of the event, shock sets in and then relieves one of the killing pain. Once recovery begins, the pain comes and goes, rises then recedes. But graciously, it's never as bad as it would have been if someone is totally conscious and cognizant throughout the whole ordeal.

I sit in my crinkled leather chair, one that is now well-worn from years of sitting, crying, curling, smiling, reading, denying, and dreaming. Each wrinkle has a story. Each crease has a memory. I hold the bundled envelopes in my lap. Perhaps twenty-five or thirty letters, each postmarked the same, most unopened until the past few nights. The envelopes vary in size and, in some instances, markings; but each holds the distinctive automated postmark circle at the top right corner of the mailing. The dates range from February through December, sporadic and in no particular pattern or sequence, as the years cover nearly two decades. But the city postmark was always constant: Lebanon, Ohio.

Flipping the corners of the top three or four letters back and forth, I read the name of the author letter by letter, with mixed feelings of either burning each envelope and its contents now— let the words inside stay covered forever—or let them reproduce inside my head as they had since last Saturday. My eyes zero in on the return-address corner. I see each letter clearly printed by hand: O-S-B-O-R-N-E. Osborne, followed by a consistent alpha-numbering sequence assigned to him and, below both, the address of the dreaded correctional institute.

Each postal product, each script, had been diverted from my address to my victim's legal advocate's office to protect me. I am forever grateful for the interception by my advocate, Sharon Gaffney, attorney-at law. Sharon had stood by me constantly through each of the legal steps, as well as the subsequent and very-much-appreciated parole denials. She brought the existence of the prisoner's letters to my attention once, after Sharon had perused a randomly selected letter. After the pardon, the bundle was presented to me with the admonition, "It's your call, but you may want to take a look at these." And the thoughts of a murderer were placed in my hands.

I had opened the first one on an isolated Saturday night, one in which I found myself dateless and comfortable in my aloneness. Thinking that the first of the letters would provide the least amount of pain, I let the written contents move from the sealed seclusion of the rain-stained envelope and into the fresh but not forgiving air of my home.

The letter was dated February 9, less than six months after his self-induced conviction. It read:

Dear Ms. Roberts,

I am very sorry. So very sorry.

That was it. Two blunt sentences and just seven words. My first reaction is one of emptiness, not for me but for the writer. The words are simple, though they did not come across as unintelligent. The basic font suggested handwritten patience. Neatness, influenced by brevity. At first, I was not going to read any more. I expect an excuse-making litany of this and that, a "poor me, I'm the real victim here" bestseller. Far from that, I feel emotionally curious and persuade myself to read one more.

After the first letter and a week's pause, I select the next letter by the date. I hold the letter in my hand. As if to maintain a historical relic, I carefully slide a metal-trimmed plastic ruler under the lip of the envelope, careful not to create a ragged edge. There is no logic for this. I am timid at best in opening each letter. In one way, it is a feeling similar to walking into your pitch-black house as a child, expecting the boogeyman to suddenly appear two feet in front of you and scare the bejesus out of you. In another way, it is a cautious respect for what is about to be revealed. If I am calm and gentle in opening up the envelope, the boogeyman might refrain from his acts of spookiness and stay for a filtered conversation. That's what this is, I think, the b-man; and if I'm careful, this will not hurt me.

Tonight I open a May-dated letter from Osborne's first year of incarceration. It is as simple as the first one, no more emphatic but just as basic. The apology, but this time, it comes with a touch more emotion. There is a vague hint of feeling appearing with each word. It reminds me of a childhood game, where I am a secret agent, and I write messages in lemon juice on small slips of paper to my counterpart, another seven-year-old classmate. Once written, each coded sentence could only be read if you were trained properly and were certified as a government agent. In reality, it meant nothing more than holding the letter up to a lamp and anyone could read the secret message. Odd, how I hadn't recalled that memory for thirty or so years. Are there secret messages here? The reflection of lemon juice and childhood, though, brings me a nostalgic comfort as I return to the correspondence from Osborne. I am a trained secret agent, and the b-man is not going to spook me.

What am I to do now? Read on? I can't help it. There is more. There is an explanation for Jake's death. Some reason, some justification—not to rationalize Osborne's actions but to fit a piece of the life puzzle in place so I can see the greater good. I don't feel it, but my faith justifies my hesitancy by convincing me that yes, there is a God, there is karma, there is a complex chronological formula. I can someday sit down and, with a divine calculator, conclude, "Ah, now I have the correct answer." The complex life mystery will be explained.

I read on.

Osborne reveals a few more sentences, worded as though to be persuasive but with a timidity to them that reflects more of a reverence than I would have originally guessed. I hold the letter up into the light and look past the words to the lemon-stained secret feelings behind it. In my mind, not in my heart, I sense that I am giving Osborne permission to enter. To enter what? I think, perplexed. My cerebral captain and spiritual first mate continue a thorough debate, as if I am trying to shake hands with myself. The fingers don't quite fit, but each hand is cooperating; each knows the other has good intentions. "Please continue," I *whisper out loud. The voice startles me back to the chair. My blue-jeaned legs curl up in the weathered leather. My words echo off my chocolate-brown sweater sleeves muffled around the backs of my hands. It's curious how I actually lift the letter up to see imaginary feelings within each word of Osborne's confession.*

I carefully refold the letter, snuggle it into the envelope, and place it on my lap. I feel a strange peace, as if I have just tucked the blanket around a sleeping child. Drowsy myself, I lay my head back against the recliner and feel myself slowly fade into a dream.

∞

The sun is a brilliant solar light, heating up the white sand of Seven Mile Beach in Rio de Janeiro. It feels therapeutic as it sneaks beyond my white-framed Bali sunglasses. A light breeze plays with loose strands of my auburn hair and causes my cheeks to feel a bit ticklish. It is a good tingling feeling, not unlike the playful teasing finger of my lover when we are alone in bed. Sensing the warmth on my skin, I stroll aimlessly along the water's edge, my tanned legs moving casually forward, thighs revealing a sun-touched tone. The air hugs the sheer cream-colored wrap around my hips. I carry sandals in one hand and gently squeeze the hand of my lover as we press barefoot outlines into the damp sand of the beach.

We walk the beach hand in hand; the strength of his fingers matches my appreciation. I sense both self-sufficiency and a dependency—an ideal tandem of harmony that two lovers enjoy as each day reveals more of our inner secrets. We are comfortable, yet each of us eagerly awaits more experiences, memory-making, and soul-felt exploration together. I love Rio, love the absence of inhibitions, the naturalness of skin, the rawness of an emotionally deeper relationship, and the alluring draw of the blue-green ocean water. I am both swimming in the waters of passion and, at the same time, floating aimlessly on the surface, each wave slowly lapping at my legs even while roaming the beach with my lover. So many emotions and too little time, I smile at myself. It is the perfect moment. I am in love.

I slowly awaken, seeing the room darkened by the sunset. My feet feel a twinge of coolness as I realize that I had drifted off after absorbing the sequential letter of May. Placing the box of letters under the walnut-stained end table near the chair, I stretch briefly and head to my familiar bed. I hope I can resume the dream, or perhaps a sequel, where my lover and I leave the beach and are in the beachside Cabana making love. As with a secret crush, I hope to influence the next dream by fantasizing consciously before I fall back to sleep.

∞

Each letter of the Osborne collection becomes a weekly appointment for her. Cyndi takes her time, never rushing quickly ahead but taking one letter at a time, patiently absorbing the transition from confessional excerpts of his emotional state into a semitransparent autobiography. Articulate and fluid, the letters evolved from quick candid blocks of revelation to a familiar diary that draws her in deeper with each reading. Damon reveals himself more with each letter, sketching an image in her mind that slowly becomes a focused fantasy. Her pulse sparks slightly with each letter she opens. Curling up into her favorite leather haven, she breathes in each written morsel as if each word is a kiss.

She recognizes her evolving and growing involvement. The "just-so" blouse, the coordinated colors, the careful selection of her slacks are part of her primping for a date with her letters, with solitude. She meticulously layers on the blush, paints on the lip gloss. Once she spent at least twenty minutes trying on four or five necklaces until she found the ideal amber-and-brown, double-looped decoration for her smooth neck, which made her feel lit up. Cyndi clings to this ritual, odd as it seems, to her rational self. She is immersed in a novel, in a true-to-life story in which a hated meeting of fate once cloaked in anger becomes an odd-colored butterfly. It is simultaneously gentle, delicate, new, familiar, and at the same time, perhaps short-lived. Each sitting evolves to a reading, each reading stimulates a dream, and each dream becomes her companion for days to follow.

By late autumn, Cyndi has perused and reread each and every letter from Osborne. His slow revelations, transparency, and—at least from what she could tell—honesty gives her an image that is at odds with her identity of herself, the grieving lover. Damon's face is transposed over the image of Jake. She whispers Damon's name with surprise, but not with guilt. Now, not only is he a common visitor to her inner sanctum of feelings, he is a constant invisible companion. In a way, this realization is no longer bizarre. Cyndi has melted into a fantasy of oneness, as in a movie that is fact-based but embellished by a Hollywood screenwriter. Cyndi is letting her mind free-fall into the drama, regardless of reality and regardless of her dissolving inhibitions.

Damon Osborne appears with her nightly, not by invitation but rather by lack of resistance. Cyndi drifts off to sleep with an anticipation that she will dream of him. She dreams of him holding her hand as they roam on the beach in Rio, or making love in a Lake Tahoe ski resort at Christmas time. On more than one occasion, she wakens to find herself aroused, only to see satin sheets kicked to the floor in restless passion, the bed looking both large and empty except for her satin pillows.

Her new lover is not a murderer. He's a convict, yes, but not a murderer. Osborne is like a friend whom you've known for years but can never really describe. Someone whom she learned to love but always sensed there was more to than meets the eye. Cyndi begins to see the progression of events that brought her forward some twenty-plus years later. The mosaic life print takes a clearer view with each passing month and letter.

∞

Cyndi absorbs each letter as Osborne, the con, had become a skillful and gifted writer. Having earned some meager dollars as a service dog trainer at the correctional institute, he was able to channel his endless twenty-four-hour days into a blend of ongoing diary-writing and exercising and educating fuzzy-haired, mixed-breed animals within the wire-framed walls. Cyndi is both drawn toward and intrigued by his revelations. His patience with the animals and quick intelligence soon earn him both points and dollars to purchase a laptop for use in his cramped abode, even though he is denied network use.

Osborne supplemented his dog-training commitment with influential letter writing. His gift would first give birth to words on the page and then mature as he became a self-therapist for rebuilding his life. Though he had first directed the content and sincerity of his letters to a prison chaplain, Osborne seceded from this nonobligatory partnership and increased his letters to the widow Roberts.

Enjoying her immersion into Damon Osborne's scripted life, Cyndi's vision is embellished by her emotional imagination. She misses not being able to share her latest fantasy, ignited by her reflection on a past Osborne writing. But she knows no one will understand. Hell, she doesn't understand it either. But with the years serving as a measure of the excursion, Cyndi can no longer turn back. Nor can she talk about her nightly fantasy trips with her lover. It is her solo flight each night, a mixture of fact-based reality spiced with her vivid imagination. She loves Damon. She even craves him.

Cyndi never longs for companionship of a wide circle of friends. Family gatherings are pleasant, though intermittent blends of holiday small talk, sprinkled with births and funerals. Her thoughts are of Damon—less intense than before, though no less frequent. It is October now, nearly three years, twenty-nine months to be exact since she opened the first letter. She imagines where he is, having read of his hopes to start a new life in the heart of Ohio. She read his early autumn thoughts when colleges kicked off a new term, and she pondered whether he returned to college to finish his finance degree. Did he ever reconcile with his father, Damon's script during a June letter? Perhaps his father had passed on by now, as Damon had mentioned once about the cancer. And consistently, Cyndi felt his maturing sincerity of remorse over his senseless act of years before.

She couldn't resist the draw to cyber search, scan through a myriad of network data banks to find his whereabouts. Cyndi had stayed in the suburb, paying off the mortgage with the funds from a life-insurance settlement. And Damon? She can only speculate, fanaticize.

There are gathering spots around the city, with numerous parks that draw dogs for walks, runs, and people-watching. An attractive and trim runner, Cyndi randomly tried out several routes in the city before settling in on a favorite park, a ten-acre one close by.

Cyndi finds herself looking at each mature man as she takes her daily jog through the park, enjoying the soft landing of her cushioned running shoes. Perhaps it is just a flirtatious nature she has, but she lets each person she sees meet her eyes with a gentle smile. Damon? No, she thinks as she pads by. Too young. Or too aloof-looking, she concludes. Each daily jog in the park just minutes from her home becomes a runway of prospective Damons. She craves his charm, or is it just an imagined trait that he has authored in her mind?

Late at night, she holds the love-warmth of each letter in her arms, curling up with a symbolic hugging as if she is with her lover. She reflects on her natural ability to create a fantasy, where she and Damon walk the beach, with Damon's older but still muscular body holding her hand. He occasionally releases her from the loving grip, reaching to pick up a bright yellow tennis ball and toss it outward. She watches the ball take no more than one hop off the damp sand before the blended-breed dog captures it in his mouth. Damon has bonded with the dog, and she with Damon.

Cyndi never completely waives the foolishness of her dreams but rather allows the make-believe life to be a source of forgiveness and healing for her. It doesn't have to make sense to her, but the personal evolution is healthy enough to be beneficial yet unreal enough to be exciting. The vividness of the relationship subsides for weeks at a time, once for nearly six months, though it never completely evaporates. She's constantly longing for more, for a refresher, for a next chapter to keep the spark of forgiveness alive and to keep her hope of a personal connection with Damon both possible and spirited. Frequently laying the letters side by side, Cyndi sees the transition of Damon into what she perceives as a patient trainer of dogs. While not the "dog whisperer," Damon's letters reflect his sense of purpose and focus as he balances his dog training and penmanship to work his way through the years of prison.

∞

Walking briskly through the park, the dog trainer sports a pale-blue long-sleeved shirt rolled to the elbows. Faded jeans with loose legs curl freely around his dirtied running shoes. The left pocket of his shirt displays a white embroidered patch that reads "Full Circle, Senior Trainer," a familiar name with local dog owners with a reputation for outstanding kennel services. On the right side of his shirt is a small brass name badge, etched in black letters. Looking a healthy but weathered forty or so, he smiles at the large blonde-streaked dog bounding by his side. The mixed offspring of a quick coupling, the foster pup is now a daily live-in with Damon. Freebie. A service-dog dropout, Freebie was given to Damon for the mere payment of vaccination and licensing fees, hence the name. In addition, its energy calls to mind the famous flying disc, which Damon throws ahead for the dog to recover.

"Oh, what a beautiful puppy!" exclaims a trim woman, pausing quickly from a perky jog to pet the friendly dog. Freebie seems to smile even with the plastic disc lodged deep in his jowls.

Damon steps up in the dusty path toward the woman, smiling at what he thinks is a chance meeting. Freebie always attracts a greeting from middle-aged female joggers who frequent the dirt runway surrounding the park. This woman is a looker, sporting a mauve and gray runner's top, edgy white-framed sunglasses, and hair stuffed stylishly up inside a university cap.

"What's his name?" inquires Cyndi. "You're so cute," she purrs as she kneels next to the playful dog.

"Freebie," responds Damon. "Freebie just popped into my mind, and it kind of stuck. My name's Damon," he continues. "And you are …?"

∞

I immediately freeze in my place. Goosebumps chill my sweat-glistened body. This is it. The voice echoes an eerie familiarization, a startling revelation. The tanned but weathered face of the tall man drills into my mind instantly. An unexpected fear and alert focus takes over me as I slowly stand up, pulling down the lower hem of my jogging top. The trickling of sweat from the mile plus of running reaches my hands, now nervous from the shock of this introduction.

Rubbing my hands on the hips of my shorts, I deliberately resist pulling off my wraparound glasses. I want to immediately run away and hide yet stay at the same time. Spontaneously, I feel like a victim again, viewing a police lineup from behind my tinted lenses that resemble a one-way mirror at the courthouse.

An explosion of thoughts accelerates through my head like the fast flipping of pages of a college reference book. I ignore the dog and peer at the solidly built man before me. Well-toned, he's clad in the trainer's denim work shirt with the name badge clearly inscribed, "Damon." I take in the scope of this strong creature, with brushed-back hair and a tailored two-day, age-dusted shadow of a beard. His image is completed with faded jeans and dust-worn leather running shoes, sockless. He'd surely turn the head of most any woman nearing by.

My blood feels hot. My heart is pounding as if it is pumping water out of a pond.

Even after imagining this meeting so many times, I am stifled. What do I say to the man who murdered my husband? It stings me that in this shock of happenstance, I can't remember my husband's name. All that consumes my mind is Damon, Damon, Damon. Dammit, *I curse to myself.* Wake up! *Looking away to avoid eye contact—even a filtered glance—I spit out a meager answer, "Gotta go."*

∞

With that, she spins away and sprints off at a pace far faster than when she had arrived. She welcomes the dust bouncing off her shoes, thighs squeezing and responding to her strides as she distances herself from the felon, her tormentor, her imaginary lover. She wants to run, run forever. She knows she can never outrun him, literally or emotionally. He is in her park, her home, her memory, and her mind. He is in her heart. Damon is in her!

∞

I bound up the steps and into my house, stripping my damp running clothes as I zip straight for the shower adjoining my bedroom. I mindlessly toss my sunglasses and cap on the bed and shake my hair free, damp from the panic-filled retreat from the park. The heated rush of spray cascades over my tingling skin as I turn on the water. I want to wash away the sweat, not from running but from my fantasies. I am confused, embarrassed, and aroused at the same time. Lifting my head back, I let the stinging water pulsate onto my face, hoping that it will be a well-meaning slap to bring me back to reality. Reality? Is it the reality that I had just come face-to-face with a murderer? Or more likely, I am hopelessly over the top in my distorted and private illusions and need a potent drug-induced therapy.

The heated water rolls down my face, shoulders, and back, finding its way to my hips and legs. I let the steamy liquid both soothe and stimulate me. Each drop is a memory, a thought, a word, a feeling. I think that if the rain of the shower continues long enough, each drop of water will start making words into complete sentences. Maybe I can read and absorb this aquatic message—that each drip will pool together to show me the definition of my feelings. The hot waterfall over my body is comforting, erotic. Like a recluse in a cabin deep in the woods, I feel secure and isolated in the shower. I try not to think but to listen. The white noise of the shower massages my mind until the message is clear to me. I need and want Damon.

Wrapping myself in a deep pile towel, I reach up to the closet shelf and pull down the box of letters. I place the box on my bed and curl into the familiar position of courtship. Well-worn now from many readings and caresses, each letter emits a lover's glow from the envelope. Like tarot cards, I deliberately place them side by side on the comforter, sensing somehow that there is a message that will guide me forward.

It is clear that forgiveness has occurred. What she had not counted on was obsession. Evenings of solitude had turned into quiet readings and reflections. Letters were absorbed over and over until she knew Osborne well as any lover. Damon is always inside her. Cyndi had always clouded this from others. No one knows the depths to which Damon resides inside her mind, her spirit, and her body. The meeting in the park was more than a coincidence; it was a telling of fortune.

Cyndi long ago dealt with the adversarial struggle of good versus evil, forgiveness versus revenge. Oddly, neither extreme gave her any form of peace from a clear heart or satisfaction from payback. It is only the close intimacy with Damon that fulfills her. This obsession consumes her day and night. She wakes with him each morning. She feels his imaginary heat upon her pillow as she fades into sleep at night. It is useless to resist. She confirms the same feeling that a drowning person has before losing both consciousness and life: it is both calm and peaceful when resistance ends. She succumbed readily and long ago to the induced high of his drug. Self-induced or not, it matters little.

Like a starstruck fan of a sports celebrity, Cyndi collects the courage to make the next move. Somehow, she senses it will be both fulfilling and horrifying. She reflects that she is leaving the womb of make-believe and risks being discarded by the star in real life. But it is her call to make, her choice, and she sets her course for a confrontation, albeit a carefully crafted one.

At the Full Circle kennel, Damon finishes the final feedings of the twenty-plus dogs at the compound. The loud ongoing conversation among the wide range of canine citizens is no more annoying than usual. He's learned to filter most of it out except for his ability to sense when a dog is in pain or suffering, which is rare, and he has an acute sense of caring in that regard. He's had a good week, with four more service dogs earning placement among those in need of a loyal and friendly pet. He's also pleased that another two of his loving retreads are scheduled for adoption by the end of the week. Looking forward to the end of his ten-hour shift, he'll soon find himself opening the back door of his car and watching Freebie jump in to give directions to Damon's house. Then it is off to the park.

Turning the corner to the front office, he pauses as he opens the door. Standing in the foyer is the woman, the park runner from three weeks ago. After his initial start, he glances up and down as if to inspect her to ensure this is indeed the fleeing jogger. His visual pat-down ends at her face, where she stands with her white in-vogue sunglasses resting comfortably above her pleasant but unexpressive face. She's impressively dressed in a white-cream blouse and modestly short skirt. The runner looks professional and on the serious side. She reflects an image of tremendous health and the confidence of someone who is hereby designed for a defined purpose. Somehow, Damon knows this isn't about a dog.

Her arms are crossed in front of her. She pauses as if waiting for Damon to approach her. Damon takes the hint and, sensing that this was not the moment to be overtly friendly, steps toward her. Alone except for the occasional beep of the phone system above the distant echoes of dog talk, the woman reaches out her hand toward Damon. It is not a gesture for a handshake, but she offers him a weathered envelope with a familiar yet painful address in the upper left-hand corner. Its ragged edges suggest that its contents have been viewed repeatedly. Damon takes the envelope, and his eyes are drawn to the postmark from

Lebanon, Ohio. The date, in now-faded postmark ink, is February 9, nearly twenty-five years ago.

Damon knows what this is and what is inside. He pulls open the torn envelope to retrieve the simple handwritten letter from its cover. His eyes flow over the powerful, sincere words that he had written many years before. Scribed in basic block letters, authored within his deep remorse, are the words *I'm very sorry. So very sorry.* And at the end is the familiar closing signature, "Damon Osborne."

Before him, to his astonishment, is Cyndi Anne Roberts.

∞

She veers into her driveway and scampers inside her house. With a rush of adrenaline, she pulls out an empty but well-worn backpack from the hallway coat closet. Inside she places a pair of light-gray running shoes with florescent stripes, a favorite pair of shorts, and a white tank top. Without hesitation, she takes the backpack to her bedroom and pulls open the nightstand drawer. The 9 mm automatic pistol warms instantly in her hand, as if it had been waiting all day to be welcomed into her travel bag. Completing her ensemble, Cyndi grabs a cap and zippers everything together. She is a mere fifteen minutes from the park, and she has a run to make.

Cyndi knows this will be the closure, the end, though she doesn't know why or how. She only knows that Damon is no longer a fictional persona of her wild and uncensored mind. He is in her and has to leave.

∞

Damon does not alter his course from the usual routine. He and the frisky dog head for the daily park rendezvous. Freebie always seems to follow a predetermined course around the park, though he'd add perhaps another half a mile of meanderings for good measure and good sniffing. It is a wonderful seventy-seven degrees, perfect for any activity that makes one happy. Damon is reflecting on the meeting with Cyndi—how it was odd to explain. Yet somehow he views it as a sign of things to come. Freebie continues his exploration, and Damon his analysis of the perplexing puzzle.

Cyndi keeps a quick pace along the park's jogging trail, her brightly striped sport shoes scrunching against the soft dirt, her breathing in a quick cadence with her legs as she runs. Her cap is low over her sunglasses, hair pulled back into a ponytail that sways side to side as it has for many years of her park workouts. The backpack shifts against her skin where the scant white tank top misses. Sweat gleams upon her skin. She is in sync now—pacing, focused, and ready.

Damon walks the gentle curve of the pathway, not paying notice to the wide ranges of shapes and sizes of people going from back to front and front to back. Had he not been deep in thought, mesmerized by the earbuds and music of the Plain White T's, he would have noticed more quickly the sexy runner coming toward him wearing white sunglasses, a university cap, and a brief tank top. Others in the park certainly notice her. She very clearly stands out wearing the backpack and running much more briskly than her contemporaries, and her well-matured legs are taking long deliberate strides.

The runner stops a mere six feet in front of Damon and his beloved dog. She flips up the white sunglasses and perches them upon the bill of her cap. Reaching around, her right hand disappears behind her back. Damon recognizes Ms. Roberts, and she looks as appealing in running gear as she did at the dog palace. His isn't sure how to greet her but pauses to let her take the lead.

Cyndi stands, plants her feet firmly, and takes a deep, hard look. Her tanned arms move upward as she draws a bead. Her eyes take on a steely look as the gun zeros in on its target. There is a stunned silence in the park, and the female soon-to-be-assassin locks on to her victim. There is no time to react, not a second to reflect, dodge, or move in any way.

Damon freezes in horror as he looks into the face of his killer. Cyndi looks at Damon Osborne, and her wet lips form very clean, emotionless words: "Pardon me." With this, she squeezes the trigger three quick times in succession.

The first two loud pops penetrate Damon as both bullets disappear into his chest. A deep red oozing covers the white embroidered patch, and the words "Senior Trainer" disappear within the scarlet. Damon never staggers, never clutches his chest, but simply collapses to the ground. In a muffled thud, he lay dead on the park pathway.

Cyndi completes her day with the last and final shot. Looking toward the clear blue sky as bystanders stare in horror, she opens her mouth and quietly but distinctly says the words, "Pardon me, Governor." The gun rises to her mouth, and her full lips suck the barrel of the killing tool. Another pop. Cyndi collapses to the ground.

The crowd of runners, walkers, and lovers overcome their shock, surrounding the death scene immediately. Cell phones pop up as alerts are made to the authorities; others continue their frantic escape from the park to secure protection. Within minutes, sirens from emergency vehicles are heard, and the stunned crowd gets ready to make the evening news as eyewitnesses.

Among the confusion and din, a lonely soul pauses near the bodies. Within two deep-brown eyes reflect the sadness of one who has lost a dear friend and the peaceful reflection toward one who is forgiven. The emotions of the moment are lost upon those surrounding the loyal dog.

Freebie sits, reflects, and waits.

Never Again

Kelly

My spine tingles, tickled by beads of sweat, as I run along Hampford Beach. My fast-dry pink runner's shirt absorbs the dampness beneath it. The soft flannel hoodie flops with each step. The prickly sensation from my black tights is invigorating and somewhat arousing. I extend another inch or so, toes reaching out, stretching my calves. My adrenaline surges and fuels an athletic impulse in my stride. My sluggish warm-up of minutes ago is now a fluid motion on the rain-glazed boardwalk. I feel the muffled sound of my stride ricochet inside my head, looking for a place to stick. Generic white earbuds, twisted numerous times to find a nesting in my ear canals, are loosely tangled with soft bouncing wires.

Melodies waft inside my mind, aimlessly, one after another. Musical rhythms push my pace. I cringe after a brisk hundred meters (at the halfway mark of my five-miler, I'm proud to say) when Michael Bublé croons about coming home, going home, something like that. The slowdown hits me, the memory of warm sunlight through a winter windshield. My legs respond sluggishly. Enough! I finger the tab on my sleeve. Michael doesn't protest; he understands. Creed steps in—a relic of the '90s but potent for the second stretch of my beach-long run.

Trickles of sweat again. My feet heat up the insides of my dusty-tan Adidas. I surge faster. Bass notes slap in time with my feet. The lead singer's screeches are stimulating though imperfect. *Whump. Whump.* Step after step. *Thump. Thump.* The song speeds on. I keep pace.

I glance at my ten-dollar wristwatch, the model that I lose once a year and buy with a 50 percent–off coupon. Too shadowy to view my time, I peer ahead in the darkness to the next amber light hovering over the runway. I expect my pace time to be close to the seven-minute mark. Last Saturday's ten-kilometer race placed me fourth in the female twenty-five–twenty-nine age group. I missed out on the top-three ribbon, but I'm still pleased with the result. Now! Creed scratches out the song. I glance at my watch under the yellowish shadow of the night, confirming my judgment that I'm clipping along in the 6:50 p.m. range.

The October air is chilly for the season here, more in flavor with my Northern Michigan roots. I'm longing for home. The skiing, the logs popping fireflies against the mesh screen, and the Mackinac fudge made by my mother are wooing me. Five months removed from Michigan, I'd pioneered here to join the staff of a regional health-care exchange, lobbying the unemployed and underemployed to sign up for government-subsidized medical benefits. My thoughts amble to my workplace and to the whole process of selling the seven different plans available.

I run briskly, my mind out of state but my feet in the Carolinas. I target a small cabana for a turnaround, knowing I can curl back for an invigorating circular workout. I remember the cabana from my summer jaunts. Modest, twenty feet per side with splintered cedar siding weathered by seasonal and yearly ocean winds, it stands alone in the darkness. The pop-open panel, whose purpose is more to shield beachcombers from sun than to provide winter security, is wired down for the off-season. The structure once housed imported booze with various clever names such as Ron Rico Gold and Old Monk. Each bottle travelled elsewhere after Labor Day, no doubt giving up its life for the sake of thirst-quenching pleasure. I scan the chain-link fence backing the bar. The barrier marks the territorial demarcation of the end of the public beach, my jogger's cul-de-sac.

A weathered sign overhead, which I had memorized but not memorialized, reads Beach Bums—Drink Till You Drop. I find the coed-seducing slogan humorous, knowing the sensibilities of the more mature residents living year-round here and the frequent patrol of the local law-enforcement team, county and state. I forgo the drinking (and driving) temptation year-round, knowing this workout will offset just six hundred calories. Burning off a piña colada would take another three miles.

I'm amused. I recognize links of a thought chain. It starts with a rock singer's lyrical tirade, how his heart is burning for love. The burning transfers itself to the heat inside my socks, making me want to peel them off and cool my feet in the ocean. OMG, the link of thoughts now has me skinny-dipping in the ocean, and I realize in my mental wanderings that I've forgotten a towel. This reminds me to put the spun-dampened towels into the dryer when I get home. Chain links. Thought links. My mind is home now, tallying a to-do list, wondering if I've missed another link somewhere. My body is nearing the cabana.

Morris

I scratch myself, pulling my hand out of my jeans. Feels likes bugs, but it's too cold for skeeters. I've been here at the local beach for three nights. This beach bar is a lonely but accessible dive for me. An angry growl erupts from my gut, ignored for nearly a day in spite of my ramblings up and down the beach. The green recycling cans are staggered signposts along the sand, but none harbor any aluminum cans to swap for quick cash. Clear bottles with brown dots of residue have teased me daily from the bottom of the huge plastic containers.

The beach is usually empty at night. Last night, a couple—guys, I think, but I didn't care—strolled the ocean's edge. Lovers? Perhaps. I'd seen it all in my thirty-some months in prison. Drugs. Beatings. Gang rapes—nearly always forced on the youngest and freshest male meat who arrive at the seventy-year-old stone castle. Scores of bartering deals going on. I'd fared well, for the most part. I traded my meager math skills to others for sexual protection from the muscle-tightened bullies of the C wing. It wasn't much of a contribution. Most didn't know if my numbers were correct or not. I had sketched out a mock budget for some con's guy's crazy business idea. His plan, sucky at best, was to recycle prison garb and make patchwork pillow covers. "Sell 'em back to the prison dicks," he announced. "Make five bucks a sale."

Moron. I'm out. He's in. Still believing the fuzzy numbers I gave him, which I scribbled out on a cafeteria napkin. I've been out less than a month now—hungry, bitter, angry, and vengeful. Sexual assault: I'd pled guilty. Broke back then and not able to make bail after a year in the city jail, I traded my constitutional right to bear arms and vote (which I never did anyway) for a three-to-five-year visit to a concrete hell. Yeah, I screwed her. I'd do it again. I slapped her once, which I regret. I'd told myself, *It ain't right*. But my rage takes over. Dad had slapped Mom around. She dealt with it—I ignored it.

During my incarceration, it was eat or be eaten, beat or be beaten. Survival came by one of two motivations: power, as a rationalization for a failed and pathetic life in the outside world, or release, the motivation to get out. We all clicked the hours off, the days, and the nearly unbearable months. I'd had a setback, sent to the hole. A thug deliberately placed a stolen dinner cup under my hard bed slab. I was given two weeks of solitary and an extension of my hoped-for early release.

My souvenirs are a few scars, one knife-induced, along with a chipped tooth, and some body art. I bartered with an inmate, allowing him to scrape an arc of bluish chain links across my left bicep. Halfway through the third link is a break, the severed link partnered with the words *Never Again*. The self-taught prison artist had misspelled the word as *agin* but was able in squeeze in an *a* after I threatened to ream him.

I was tempted to spite the judge and have the *f-bomb* inked on my other arm. I cancelled that order. The old fart in his baggy black robe gave me a lecture about the law, morals, and force. Regardless of my court pleading, the words *forceful, unlawful, carnal, knowledge*—the legal elements of rape—became part of the judge's pontification. So yeah, I fucked her. But the word now haunts me. Habitually, I use it, then His Honor's words come streaming back: "Forceful, unlawful…"

My gut gurgles again. I'm also thirsty, my mouth swollen from dehydration. Homeless, I discovered this old beach bar a few days ago after being kicked out of a flophouse apartment. I didn't register as a sex offender, didn't check into the parole office. I forgot (or ignored) the inscription on my arm muscle. The solitude along the beach is beneficial and, much to my need, nocturnal. I'll venture out to the fringes of town in a few hours. Certainly, there'll be a leftover burger or a few castoffs from a restaurant to tide me over another day. I fantasize about a hot meal, a soft pillow, a shot glass of whiskey, and sex.

Kelly

I blanked out again and again during the examination, which was now about a month ago. The humiliation was nearly equal to that caused by the attack, but for a different reason. I was angered at my stupidity for running myself into the corner, for jogging into the blackness. The darkness of the cabana's turnaround was ripe for an attack. Only in the movies, I'd thought. Had I only…

The physician administering the rape kit was even-tempered and professional. She was emotionally gentle, which I appreciated, as if she had experienced the same crisis as me. With my legs spread and thighs opened, I tolerated her cold hands. I shivered repeatedly through the entire process. No family members anxiously waited outside, only a counselor to probe me verbally and sketch the event.

I can't tell you if it was quick. It hurt. He stunk. He was strong but seemed to weaken quickly, as I did. But his fading was not, regretfully, quick enough for me to escape. Perhaps if I'd had one more surge of energy—a mile less in my workout—I could have repelled his stale body. But one less mile and I would have been home safely, wouldn't I? Had I only…

I'd approached the cabana lost in thought. I saw a movement, a distraction, a dark flash of something. The force was both a push and a pull. A blow to my ribcage deflated my lungs. My face hammered into the scratchy plywood siding. I felt a quick sting of the tearing of cheek skin. Then the pull. My shoulder joint dislocated from its socket. I was slammed to the unforgiving boardwalk. Muffled grunts echoed in the damp air. My stifled hearing was muzzled by earbuds; one wiggled free, falling.

A blow to my kidney stunned me. Screaming pain exploded out of my mouth, sounds that could not be spelled or replicated. Greasy-feeling fingers, almost slippery, squeezed around my neck. A fist pounded my shoulder twice. Right or left? "I don't know," I told the detective. The blows' impact radiated pain across my upper back; left and right merged into one region of horrible pain. I writhed, twisted, pushed, resisted, and screamed. Cold fingers tethered my waistband. Freezing air burnt my buttocks as my leggings were pulled down my thighs. Hard knees pinched, a hard vise against my ribcage. My feet kicked fitfully and futilely. A shoe rolled off my foot.

I squirmed, twisted, battled, and stretched. If I had only. The link of fears and if-onlys gathered together and hit me with a steely force. I drifted, faded, collapsed into unconsciousness.

The waves lapped over the sand, oblivious.

∞

The call came quickly, a Tuesday morning about two weeks after the attack.

Relief? I'm not sure. Numbness? Yes, to some degree. More so a garbage bag of emotions in spite of my mind's pleading to toss it at the curbside.

The lineup proved useless. My body's rearview mirror was busted in the attack, I'd bitterly complained to the detective. Quickly apologizing, I backed off due to the counselor's calm coaching. I was eager to learn more of the arrest from the detective.

The maggot was apprehended quickly, spotted rummaging through cans in the back of a hotel. A third-shift service worker alerted security. Detained for questioning, the local sheriff's department kept him for the night. Vagrancy, trespassing, and then the criminal automated data system—CJLEADS in North Carolina—announced the aggressor's felon status and the warrant for his arrest: parole violation. The detective assured me he had enough to send the convict back to the farm.

I should find this consoling, though it comes back to me as a hopeful promise rather than a guarantee. Perhaps I'm thinking *bought the farm*, which gives me greater satisfaction. Distracted by fantasies of vengeful retaliation, I am not thinking clearly. I shake the thoughts away so I can absorb more.

The alleged, Michael Morris, aged thirty-one, is an admitted and convicted sex offender. Detective Mack Ryan put the pieces together for me with exaggerated self-confidence. The rape kit produced undisputed confirmation of penetration. The sample retrieved was a perfect match to Morris. Ryan also detailed the constant rubbing by Morris of his left bicep by fingering the links of his crude tattoo. The cabana shared its symbolic testimony as well, giving up Morris's tattered sleep roll, an empty liquor bottle, and missing since the attack, my left shoe. "Can we shoot him now?" I begged. "What about penal amputation?" A hand on my shoulder from Kim, the counselor, eased the sting of my words. I retreated back into my chair.

Morris

I'm too tired to curse, too weak to protest. The feeble attempt I made to elude capture was an embarrassment, totally ineffective. I couldn't even muster up bragger's rights for some clever tactic I had used to delay my arrest. I was nailed behind the Hampford Sands Hotel, where I was scrounging for food. My gut was so shriveled, I would have been grateful just to chew on a rib bone or two. I'd just choked down two stiff but buttered dinner rolls—fortunate toss-outs from a near miss with the garbage disposal. The bread helped.

Some rent-a-cop had approached me, his belly hanging over a plastic-looking belt, displaying a cheap corroded badge. I told him to go to hell. The punk guard startled me by pulling a gun—a *gun*! He then flipped open a mobile phone and claimed to have poked in 911 with a pudgy finger. "Easy, dude," I protested. Pledmon—or some name like that—not only stood his ground but expanded it. I'd like to say that time stood still. The opposite was true. A sheriff's car crunched around the corner of the hotel almost immediately, the driver aggressive and thirsty for a collar. Must have been a slow night for the locals.

"Shit, man!" Like a jerk, I cursed without thinking. My mouth shot in gear before my brain engaged. I braked my mouth immediately, knowing I'd travelled this criminal path before and thus shouldn't add to my dilemma. The officer, Deputy Prick or something like that, spun me around, forced a backward ninety on my right arm, and bent me over a steel trash container. The you-know-what's-coming-next words, "You have the right…," rattled into my ears without a personal invitation from me. Reality hit me: it's over. I thought of the runner, the girl I had humped.

"Forceful, unlawful…Unlawful, not entitled to," I could hear a judge preaching.

∞

Sitting on the cold steel bench, I shivered from the cold, belly bulging from an aluminum platter full of gray gravy, hard biscuits, and something yellow resembling eggs. I washed it down with weak tea, pondering my next domicile. I knew I was screwed. The Big House was mocking me, saying my bed was made, "come and sleep in it." In spite of my hesitant and weak attempts to negotiate, I had little leverage. Rape, violation of parole, failure to register as a sex offender, theft, threatening a law-enforcement officer— hell, I didn't remember that. Since when is "I'm gonna kick your ass" a threat? Everybody says it.

I spent nearly forty-five minutes hand-scribing a confession, one of the times when it's just like on *Law and Disorder*. I had one condition: that it would not be videotaped and that only my public defender could be present when I wrote out the titillating details. I didn't give a damn. The PD was a hot number from the class of '95, I guessed. I figured I may as well lick some eye candy while I signed my way back to prison. Oddly, she didn't lecture me. Aware that I was toast, she surmised that I was simply a file to close out, like the other ninety or so misguided folks in her caseload. My case, with complimentary confession, was an easy scratch-off for her.

The cheap orange coveralls I was issued covered up my tattoo. Strangely, I hadn't thought of it until now. What I had hoped to be a mantra was now simply a stain on my arm. I aimlessly pondered the past few weeks, meandering though the pile of crap in my head. Nothing seemed right or wrong. I replayed the booze, the hard ground, and the girl.

The PD asked me how I felt about what I'd done; I said nothing. I meant that. I said, "Nothing. The opportunity was there. I took it." "Pathetic," she muttered. *Pathetic*. I didn't consider that preaching. Perhaps there's something to her comment.

The process of documenting my return to my former cell—about a two-hour drive away—goes more quickly than I had hoped. Worse still, I'll be put in a county sheriff's car, maybe Deputy Prick's, to be driven back. I can't do this. Not again. Never again. No.

Kelly

Soreness persists. Determination replaces anger over my attack, my rape. My counselor is persistent in the message of strength, focus, and persistence. Revenge is in remission, dampened now with the love and support of those closest to me. Others only know what was revealed in the local online news and regional television presentations, twice last month and once this week as Morris's confession became public knowledge. "Focus on the what, not the why," my advisor said. For weeks, just as she said, I had looked in the mirror, cursing, "Why? Why me? Why didn't I turn at the two-mile mark? Why didn't I see him—or at least *expect* him—behind the cabana?"

My counselor wisely conveyed to me that the struggle with the whys comes first. The conflict with this sense of victimization can linger for what seems like an eternity. "Focus on the whats," she added. "Work toward your desire to survive." Slow agonizing days of pondering why did drag on. Now I look in the mirror with a determination to shape and influence my future. A wise counselor she is, and quotable.

The whats are not defined by revenge, though I deeply yearn for soothing justice. Whats are woven into the fabric through calm and comforting words of love, hope, health, strength, and survival. A distraction to my effort—and surely an unneeded complication—is my counselor's admonishment for revelation, to share my traumatic ordeal within a private setting of other victimized women. I've been encouraged to share my story. Venting is cleansing, some said. I struggled with this quandary: the guilt of refusing the overture, which conflicts with my need for respected privacy.

Stories exist, though not many, where the victim approaches the perpetrator to ask the question why. Morris is cold, hard, stupid, and remorseless. His sick reply would most likely be, "Why not?" Perverted bastard! Payback hunger is creeping into my thoughts, rent free. I purge the temptation, banish the emotion.

The district attorney approached me, laying out the confession and the corresponding impact. We discussed the arrangement in detail. He was merciless toward Morris, respectful but distant with me. Five years of incarceration is guaranteed, no early release, with Morris being ferried up to the most secure wing at the big house nearly one hundred miles away. The DA's legal partner, a mature elderly lawyer with thirty-some years with the county, added that my request for the felon's dick removal was considered but denied by the judge. I smiled at his attempt at levity. The assistant's intent is pure, though he will never understand the terror—the nightmares and loss of intimacy—that I suffer. As a teammate and supporter through the entire legal process, I forgave him.

Morris

I hate these steel bars, this cold concrete. I'm suffocating in this cramped jail cell. Time is running out. I'm not scared, not angered anymore. Complacency is not the word, which is not giving a damn. Focus, yeah, I'm *lasered in* to what I need to do—*now*. I'm bitching at myself over the whys, not why I *did* the girl, but why she showed up when I wanted to be left alone at the beach, away from cops and parole jerks.

I'm a loser, but I know what I'm going to do.

My waking time is mostly after dark now. I hate being awake during the day to hear the echoes, clanking and yelling of pissed-off people at the jail. I lay still on the hard cot until my guess is that it's three in the morning. A single bulb-light fixture domes down from the hallway ceiling. The dome harbors a cream-colored coiling bulb of sixty watts that creates eerie shadows. The government-grade light is marginal for viewing, adequate for concealing. Stripped of my weathered clothes, I have only baggy boxers and a starchy jumpsuit to cover my skin. I was unsuccessful in swiping a spoon or fork from the dinner serving. Too obvious, I pondered. The theft would be sensed immediately, and the jackass jailor would be on alert. No razor. Mirrors are nothing but scratched reflective plates on each cell wall, six inches square.

Medications are moot. I wasn't even good at faking illness in school or prison. The best I could hope for is low-grade aspirin; that wouldn't so much as cause a belch. Self-mutilation is hard with nothing to work *with*. Self-elimination is easy when there's nothing to live *for*. Creativity thrives in prison. Games are invented, cellmates partner to start minibusinesses using cigarettes as moolah, muscle as security. Products are made from every conceivable resource.

I dig into my brain for any resource—what could a convict do, short of attacking a guard? I get chills thinking back on my hard time. The rage sets in again; my pulse shoots rapidly. I'm ready to take anybody on again. But sucker punching a prison guard would only result in a painful beating, being shackled, and dumped in isolation for weeks. I'm not sure the county jailors would go that route. Regardless, the punishment would leave me battered. The deputies would lie about what happened, no doubt. Sheets are banned, a settlement in some lawsuit where an inmate hung himself. *Don't hold your breath*, I think. *Because it doesn't work.* The body has no voluntary way to hold air in the lungs until oxygen evaporates. Natural muscular reflex will spit the remaining air, causing an inrush of lifesaving breath.

Find a way. *Any way!*

I hear the clatter of belts, guns, handcuffs, and doors. Shift change, distraction. I feather my finger around the flat county-issued pillow, spotting a wear hole in the cover. It's nearly quarter-sized; I can force a finger into the frayed opening. Pushing deeper into the fold, I grab the surrounding cloth to pull and hopefully separate the cover from its foam pad. A couple of times, no luck. The hole is elongated now. Two of my fingers can be forced into the stubborn but growing opening.

Biting down hard on the cloth cover, I clench my teeth in a fitful tug, a lion shredding its prey. There's a crack, a pop. Pain shoots through my jaw. I release, spitting a tooth out to the concrete floor, bloodless. Round two fails. The third time is no match for the bullheaded pillow. Using a painful jerk, a strip of ragged cloth finally rips free from the cover. The exposed foam stinks of human hands, snot, and semen. I'm disgusted by the small segment of cloth I have to work with. *Be resourceful*, I think.

I step up to the barred gate of my cell. My jaw is throbbing. My lips are swelling. Cursing comes out as "bluck, gob blam it." Glancing down the jail's hallway, I see the despised brown-shirted deputy jailors, yellow and black patches on their sleeves labeling their allegiance to the county's justice system. The younger deputies, smirking, retrieve clipboards and sit down to mouse-driven old computers. Their arrival makes my gut churn. Time to take over the head count of the jail, I presume. Laughter, muted though audible, is followed by distractions of clicked logins, checking in of weapons, and jokes about tonight's dinner menu.

Hurry! I twist the pillow tatter into a tight curl. The gag is the length of my hand yet long enough to allow a force-feeding. The stinky rag goes into my mouth, two fingers press downward as a spontaneous cough explodes. The gag loosens. I stumble to the bed, striking my knee, the pain as dull as the sound of the impact. Rolling onto my back, I stop at a prone position and repeat the process. Opening my mouth, the cloth is shoved in again, now wet with slobber. Smothering takes three minutes. What about choking? People die in restaurants from ham sandwiches and a spoonful of rice. *Michael boy, you're going down. Don't screw this up.*

The taste is better now, more welcoming as my mouth dampens the cloth, making it easier to swallow. I choke, reflect, push, gag, and attempt to swallow. My lungs are compressed; breathing is snuffed. No longer able to swallow, I pinch my nostrils and feign a deep inhale. Covering my nose tighter with my right hand, I switch my suffocation effort to my left hand, fingering the choke deeper down my throat.

There is nothing to release. My lungs are a void with no reprieve from the cell's stale air. Darkness shrinks into blackened circles, enlarging and shrinking again as my pupils adjust to a loss of consciousness. This shouldn't take long. No chains on me when they drive me back to prison. Never again.

Kelly

My reaction? Shock, I guess.

The news blasts me with a flood of other feelings. I have yet to process what happened; it's surreal. Morris was found dead of self-induced suffocation at 3:45 a.m., Monday, less than twenty-four hours before his excursion back to prison. I was given some filtered details, devoid of explanations as to how this could have happened. Deputies were suspended, with pay, pending an inquisition. The body was discovered still warm. EMTs failed to revive the felon's dark heart or reinflate his perverted lungs.

Thankfully, I have limited replays of my attack, though more than a few times an expanded sequel has haunted my sleep, coming to me as horrific nightmares. Conversely, I play a contrasting scene in my mind, morbid curiosity perhaps, but very human. This scene, however, is one where I've had a hand in pushing the gag down Morris's throat. While the thought of his DNA sickens me, the task of offering the last push is gratifying. More than once, I envision flipping the switch to Ol' Sparky: death by electrocution, Mr. Morris. Other times, I have pushed the first of three needles into his body to see his life slip away. In this illusion, I am given credit for utilizing unique entry points for the fatal needles. Vicarious execution, I surmised. While the imagery doesn't cause me to fist-bump my counselor, I am serenely accepting of the convict's self-induced fate. I am, after all, a survivor, offering a thumbs-up to his demise, following a symbolic flipping of my middle finger.

Groundskeeper

Burnt grass blankets the acreage of the cemetery. Slopes of the rolling graveyard are patchworked with drab markers by the dozens. A lonely crab apple tree, neglected for years, serves as a signpost to Potter's Drive, marking the final home of the delinquent, the ignored, the poor, or the criminal. Small plastic funnels stick out of the markers, empty except for the periodic appearance of fast-weaving spiders. Flecks of dried grass stick to the markers from a hurried groundskeeper weed-whipping through the grave sites.

The marker at a secluded site is the same vanilla grade as its distant neighbors: K-Mart cheap, a flat composite tribute barely a foot square, and pressed unevenly on the sod of the grave.

A woman jogger, trim and tanned, adjusts her earbuds and then tugs her pink jogging top down around her waist. Her Adidas's reflector stripes, flashing in the afternoon sun, pound the gravel-coated pathway with a *whoosh, whoosh, whoosh*. Her face is burnished by determination. Her body is fluid and graceful as she paces through the cemetery. The runner's strides are rhythmic, even, and full of purpose. The sunrays glisten on her skin. Her image is one of calmness tempered with a sense of purpose. A familiar visitor. She knows the way, though groundskeepers claim they only see her perhaps once a year. An anniversary of a lost husband perhaps? A memorial to a lost brother?

The runner curls to the right branch of the trailway, slowing to a walk at plot number C-FS12, according to the cemetery office's plot map. Her purpose is clear. Her intent unknown as she approaches a lonely and weathered horizontal marker. Approaching the site, she reaches into her hoodie and retrieves a black marking pen. Breathing deeply, she seems to gather her thoughts while she grinds her athletic shoes into the sparse grass of the grave. Pulling the marker cap off with her teeth, she kneels down and inscribes a tribute to the deceased. The secondary epitaph is simple and clear, shadowing over identical words inked one year earlier.

Concluding the gesture, the runner snaps the cap back in place, returning it to her pocket. Stepping back to admire her artistry, she turns to resume her run out of the cemetery. Pausing before her first step, she leans her head to the side. Her lips hurl a whitish ball of spit. The wad splatters onto the foot of the grave.

A weathered groundskeeper, tenured for more than a decade, absorbs the ritual and stops his raking. The cemetery's lone visitor runs quickly, evaporating through the open front gate for another year. Reflectively, he strolls over to the grave, both with reverence and curiosity, to read the plaque. Below the carved name of Michael Morris, April 13, 1979–May 1, 2010, are the inked words, *Never Again*.

Deer, Sir

The cold familiarity of crisp air hits Burlin McClusky as he pushes his size-eleven feet into the faded all-weather canvas boots. Tugging the speed laces, he snugs them to a comfortable tightness around his thick ankles. Grunting a bit as he dons the footwear, he stretches up, slightly winded from the compression of his beer-induced belly pressing against his thighs. Burlin pauses, catching a brief breath of air, and stretches his back, leaning forward slightly. Not hearing the muddled pop of relief, he leans in reverse. The welcomed sound comes, almost mimicking the sound of milk on kid's cereal, as he finishes the last and only step of his morning calisthenics.

Burlin pulls up the sleeves of his heavy camouflaged coveralls and presses the fiber-hooked zipper to seal him from the morning chill. Pulling one of three leather caps off a crusted, galvanized hook in the shed, he drops it on top of his greasy hair and prepares to make his daily excursion into the forty-two-acre woods at the back of his house.

Closing the door of the bright but weathered painted shed, he walks around to the sliding door. It opens into a twenty-by-thirty-two-foot storage garage. He tugs the heavy door sideways. Filtered and sleepy daylight smacks against the darkness as cool air flows into the barn. Barely dusk, he flips the light switch on and sees the glow of a dusty sixty-watt bulb light up the footage. Burlin kicks a patch of faded yellowish straw out of his pathway and makes his way to a muscular all-terrain vehicle.

Burlin is enamored with the quad ATV. Made just a state away in the southern edge of Michigan's Upper Peninsula, he bought it new three years ago as the hottest model on the market. Made by rough-talking but hardworking Yooper craft workers, the hunting vehicle is both durable and powerful. Dubbed the Hilltopper and manufactured by Terrain-Gain, the monster sports a deep-olive and drab-beige mosaic paint job, with knobby tires wide enough to add pain to anything that catches underneath them. The Hilltopper sports a two-hundred-cubic-centimeter engine and spins a circle of less than six and a half feet in spite of its size. Burlin rides it hard and puts it away wet, as the old-horse analogy goes, and takes to the woods buggy like it is his best friend. Best mechanical friend, save for his elevated all-wheel-drive pickup truck, which is aging faster than its fifty-some-thousand miles.

The burly McClusky, a former Hilltopper himself as a member of the Western Kentucky University football team, swings his six-foot-five-inch frame onto the quad and mounts to ride to treed acres. The four-coil springs groan slightly from impact as nearly three hundred pounds of human beef and hunter's clothing partner for the ride into the deer-speckled woods.

With a flick of the key, the engine sputters to life, momentarily clouding the barn with a puff of bluish-gray smoke. The odor from the engine is as familiar as the stink of his sweat after a hunt, filling his nostrils with an alpha-masculine and somewhat arousing scent. Burlin twists the throttle back and forth to heat up the Hilltopper and edges forward, releasing the clutch to move out into the emerging daylight.

Burlin rolls the quad to a stop at the back porch of the house. A decent home, it is an older three-bedroom relic that hovers close to the ground in the typical ranch-style footprint of thirty years ago. Once belonging to his father, Robert, the modest homestead became Burlin's after an untimely death in a car accident a few years ago. A large deer had bounded in front of Robert's sedan on his way home from third shift, thudding against the hood then bouncing against the windshield. An experienced and savvy driver, Robert was accustomed to the presence of deer in the roadways during the November mating season. But this collision was no match for Robert, the older Chevy, and the darkened roadway with marginal reflectors at the asphalt's edge. The collision of the three-ton car against the huge animal—estimated to be over 350 pounds—was dynamic. The result, though, was not as gross as one could have expected. The deer was tall enough that the brunt of the hit was against the animal's muscular upper shoulders. A last-second leap by the buck gave it a sliding motion onto the top of the car. Its antlers shattered the windshield, scattering particles onto the dashboard and startled driver.

Robert was familiar with the amber glow of a deer's large eyes at night. He reacted to its huge leap onto the roadway and into the path of his car. But the impact, while significant, was only a contributor to Robert's demise. While the driver's quick reflexes avoided a direct hit, the shock of live venison hitting steel shot a stinging pain through the left side of Robert's chest. Hitting the brake hard with his left foot, he immediately brought up his right hand across the stabbing pain of his failing heart.

He screeched the car to a stop, feeling the cold air smack his face from the opened and crumbling windshield. He spontaneously thought, *Where's the deer?* while he fell quickly into shortness of breath, loss of consciousness, and a quick death from cardiac arrest.

∞

Burlin misses his father, a rugged soul with whom he hunted frequently. According to reports, the death of his father was coincidental to the deer collision, partnered with only a short duration of pain. The investigating state trooper surmised that the large buck had survived with modest injuries and found its way back into the coverage of huge oak, hickory, and maple trees after impact. Rumors and legends started after the accident as no trace of the huge animal was ever found as far as a carcass. But pieces of the broken antler at the scene of the venison-vehicle wreck suggested a trophy head of sixteen points and a rack width of some four feet.

Burlin thirsts for the deer. Not out of revenge for the untimely death of his father but for the euphoric high he could get by seeing such a magnificent creature. The talk around the local county is the large red deer, which is not native to the Midwest, could no doubt be the largest ever bagged in the last two decades, maybe ever. A memorial fund was started among the local hunters in honor of his father and had grown to five thousand dollars. The cash booty is a prize for the avid hunter who brings the big deer down. The trophy will be massive, and each day, he envisions luring the mighty buck into the crosshairs of his shotgun.

Leaving the four-wheeler warmed up, Burlin pushes the wooden kitchen door open and fakes wiping his feet on the dirty throw rug. Grabbing the small plastic cooler—labeled with the scratched but visible logo of the region's largest bank—the hunter takes the prepackaged snacks and grabs an extra can of beer for departure.

"I'm hitting the woods, Linda," Burlin calls to his sleepy wife, who is still curled up in the adjoining master bedroom under three layers of quilts. He always makes it a point to let her know he is heading out, even though it is barely six in the morning.

"Be careful, babe," she murmurs. "And leave the beer alone."

"Okay," Burlin echoes and pulls the door shut with his boot, venturing into the early dawn. Popping the tab on the can, he gulps a mouthful of the cold brew and swings onto the purring Hilltopper. The seasoned hunter glances at the pump-action Remington 11-87 shotgun to ensure that it is snugly strapped down. He touches the flashlight, first-aid kit, and the spare water bottle, each a resource for a four-hour stay in the depths of nature. Satisfied that he is well provisioned, Burlin takes another swig, guns the engine, and heads for the semidarkness of the country wilderness.

∞

Burlin feels a brief surge of heat as he repeats his muscle-clenching exercises ten feet off the ground in his handcrafted tree blind. To some, it's a killer's tree house; to a hunter, it's a perch. By intensely clenching each muscle in his body and holding it for ten seconds, he builds up a surge of warmth. It takes three consecutive cycles before the benefit comes. The routine never helps his hands though, and he frequently slips off the thick gloves to blow on his fingers. The bone chill makes it challenging to sit and wait.

Deer are grazers, extremely quick when spooked, and can bound away almost with the blink of an eye. Slowly foraging for food, tempted by the crunch and flavor of acorns, the animals meander in the woods while constantly grazing. This wanderlust is supplemented by the sexual passion of female deer in heat; the rugged desires of bucks prime each of them for mounting at any time.

The wait is part of the intrigue. Time is not measured here by minutes or hours but by the reward of bringing down a solid animal-athlete who ventures within range of the well-equipped hunter. The deer population—regardless of species—comes with a superb sense of smell. Each has eyes placed wide enough to take in a vision of a 150 degrees and acceleration that puts most human runners to shame.

The typical hunter comes manned with a shotgun and scope, as is Burlin. The scope is designed to bring a distant tiny speck of brown into the hunter's view, making it appear twenty feet away. Burlin's Remington is his favorite. Weighing in at just over six pounds, it packs a wallop and carries poly-tipped slugs with an ideal barrel length of twenty inches. The impact of the ammunition can carry the killer slug nearly twelve hundred feet per second, a bit slow, but it ensures reasonable straightness for many yards—even when allowing for the wind. Excluding the Hilltopper, Burlin is priced out at nearly two thousand dollars in equipment and licensing fees. And here he sits, ready to pop a cap on the first meandering buck that comes into view.

Burlin plays by the rules. Baiting, the practice of goading animals to come forward with apples or other tantalizing treats, is outlawed in public hunting areas; but to Burlin, this is verboten even in his own woods.

Though aggressive in his personality, he tries to be patient. He could drop a smaller deer and had passed on a few in the past two weeks. He's waiting for the big one, the sixteen-pointer that now may have grown to twenty, to roam into the McClusky acreage. Dubbed Big Ben by the locals following the death of his dad, the legendary deer had been spotted—or at least rumored sightings were reported—in the past two weeks. Burlin thinks of his dad, the prize money, bragging rights, and his collegiate competitive spirit. He pushes his left leg forward to stretch out and is tempted to reach for another beer. He thinks better of it, not out of concern for the buzz but rather because he wants to avoid the echoing snap of the pop-top within the haven of trees. A snap sound like that in the woods can be heard three acres away.

The hunter waits. And waits.

∞

Linda steps out of the warm cocoon of the shower, shaking her head gently to let the last trickles of water fall from her shoulder-length hair. Naturally dark, she had highlighted her hair with playful streaks of blond. She keeps the look even when it has fallen somewhat out of fashion. The style was still good on her even with the darkening of colors by the shower. Linda has a few flaws by nature, a few marks by design, but she accepts it as one package. She wraps the plush cream-colored towel around her to capture the remaining heat.

She gingerly touches the violet and blue circles on her wrists and thighs, newly arrived since her latest intimacy. The dull pain is notable now, but oddly, it wasn't at the time. The coloring is more vivid now, the hurt bearable. There were no soft touches, no safe words used—only aggressive interruptions when she tried to quietly protest the moves by her husband, actions that were borderline consensual and frequently regrettable. She rides with the habit, having never known anything different as Burlin was her only lover. Who defined natural? It was his power that wooed her, his power to which she continuously submits. Does she really have a choice? She isn't sure.

Linda never had temptations to explore outside her marriage, though extreme sensations continuously permeated her flesh. Appeasing her conscience, she rationalized that the erotic chills were not of her doing but came naturally. Thus, fantasies were expected, frequent but not totally welcomed. Enticements surrounded her—such as Paul Edwards, the former basketball coach who resigned and took a job as an auditor following his divorce.

There's also Darren Henson, strong and athletic who is the confident manager of the electronics department at Target, who more than once offered her sizeable discounts on merchandise that were never advertised. *Single*—dropping this fact to her at a teacher-parent meeting—Darren was seen driving by in his burgundy F-100 as recently as yesterday. The truck didn't catch her eye as much as his dusty beige leather jacket. A trademark of sorts, an image. As is his slight limp, the penalty of a car crash years before.

The driver's image dissipated in her mind. She is aware of another clear day in rural Indiana. Linda still enjoys the solitude of being thirty miles out from both Vevay and Brookville yet snuggled close to the well-known fishing and boating recreational areas. She and Burlin both enjoy Indiana and had settled here a few years ago following her graduation from college and her acceptance of a teaching job at the largest grade school in the county.

Burlin had lucked out too. Though he had ended his collegiate football days due to injury, he was still able to work through the degree-program years before they met and then follow her to Vevay as a new-car salesman. Collectively, they partner well on her modest but steady money. Burlin's size gives him a sales style that borders on intimidation. Thus, he is able to keep a top-five sales status at the dealership. In addition, the flexible hours let him spend time in the woods.

She is enjoying her third year at the school; the job balances out her life. Teaching is natural to her, though she shows up to class wearing carefully selected long-sleeved blouses when her nighttime activities leave morning reminders. It's the price to pay for a climax, she reflects. And she harbors thoughts of embarrassment if any of the youngsters quiz her on what had happened. She is careful with her arm movements, wincing once in a while at the pain. With a somewhat strange longing, Linda looks forward to the next rendezvous at home.

The household arrangement works for them, having received the inheritance of the country ranch home, barn and garage, and thus, the favored absence of a mortgage. The acreage is nice, as is the solitude. Opting out of having children, the couple survives well in the country. Linda enjoys summers off from teaching, and Burlin hits the woods with his shotgun as each season allows. Linda is grateful, healthy, and as most say, very nice-looking. She finds herself having what she needs but, once in a while, fantasizes about what she doesn't have. Burlin is good to her as a rule, though a bit rough at times. He has a football player's ego that often has to be squeezed in to get through the door. Lately, all he talks about is this Big Ben thing, of bringing down the gigantic buck whose legendary status is not beyond belief.

Yeah, Linda thinks, *Burlin is good to me*. Whether he is good *for* her is something different. But she pushes the thought out of her consciousness. She drops the towel to the floor and selects a pair of pink panties to wear. Pausing in the filtered rays of the morning sun, she massages her soft skin and healing bruises with her favorite lotion. As she soothes her thighs, she breathes in the fragrance of apple blossoms. From the double-wide window of the bedroom, she can see the back acreage, the woods, and the curve of the gravel driveway that leads to the hunter's enclave. This is no man cave for Burlin, but a haven. It is a place for him to escape with his craving to win. Or perhaps it is his craving to kill. Linda pauses at the window, feeling fresh and uncertain, wondering what lies within the mystery of the trees—and the roadway out front.

∞

The famous deer moves randomly through the McClusky forest, intermittently sniffing the air. Big Ben lifts his adorned head with majestic pride to survey the gently rolling hillside, mottled with large oak trees. Now thirteen years old, the mighty buck sports a legendary antler rack of twenty-two points. The deer's crown stretches its fingers more than four feet from tip to tip. As leader of the herd, Ben traditionally ventures off on his own, seeking out clearings to find morsels of food where his huge-head burden is less problematic. Still strong and virile, Ben is the father of some two dozen offspring in the past two seasons alone. The leader is never challenged by others, though time is shrinking the size of his Southern Indiana kingdom. Age is wearing down his ability to move as he once did.

Though many local Vevans claim to have seen him, Ben is clandestine and instinctually a survivor. Bearing a distinct scar in the shape of a scripted letter *Z* just below his left eye, he is still a magnificent champion. A survivor of a major car crash two years ago, he suffered a severe cut from the windshield impact. In addition, the buck had broken his right front leg, which healed imperfectly but securely in spite of his age. He walks with a limp that is more pronounced during a trot. But the strong aged buck is still fast and furious when needed. Ben is still the king stud, and no cocky young buck has yet lowered Ben's status as father of the group. Size matters in the animal kingdom, and sex leading to offspring is the power punch that keeps Ben number one after all these years.

Ben roams forward, sniffing, nibbling, and circling in large circumferences within the woods. Color-blind by birth, as are all deer, he is limited in his ability to see detail but uses his sense of smell to ferret out danger or rewards of food. His sense of smell spurs nature's lust for breeding. Flexing his massive shoulders, he twitches his skin and continues to roam. As are all mammals', this male species' existence is centered within the core of a simple survivor universe: food, fighting, and sex.

∞

Burlin the hunter lets his eyes float across the shadowy woods, glancing forward a hundred yards or so then back to the area just ahead of him. Deer spotting is more art than science. He knows that prey is often spotted by random accident. You can't wish a deer into your visual spotlight. It's best to let nature take its course and then be alert enough to focus in when nature randomly gives a patient hunter a break. Even on a lucky day, where a grateful hunter may see more than one of the beautiful animals, the likelihood of a clean, close shot is modest at best.

While some may see this activity as cruel, it is not a sport as some testosterone-fueled guys claim it to be. Hunting is a not a game, a sport, or a competition for the avid participant. The avid participant is one who also communes with nature, respectfully playing a small role in the cycle of life, and who consumes what is taken down. Deer-hunting is not killing for the price of a hunting license; it is sourcing from the surplus of the population. At least that's what Burlin was taught when he attended a two-day, state-required hunting symposium as part of the licensing process. Supplementing his clear conscience, he doesn't bait with food, but he does take advantage of musk fragrance to draw selected deer closer to his hunting stand.

Burlin waits patiently as the sun continues to rise, warming his face and hands. He peels back a layer of his outer coating, zipping each strip as silently as he can to avoid alerting a wandering deer. He is perhaps a half hour from calling it off for the morning. Though deer graze almost continuously, they are prone to early dawn and mid-dusk ventures out to eat. Rarely can a hunter get a takedown opportunity in late morning. Live venison on the hoof is not prone to scheduling brunches for the benefit of its potential killer. Burlin is adept at rattling, the art of simulating sounds of wrestling deer with clashing antlers in the hopes that the sound of a good fight will draw the trophy buck toward him.

So the burly hunter sits, lifting his shotgun to peer through the scope in hopes he can perhaps spot a reddish-brown mix of living hide among the tall timbers of his miniforest. Seeing nothing, he lowers the powerful weapon down to his knees and lets it rest again.

Rubbing his eyes, the hunter begins to feel drowsy. Waiting for the modest deer population at his country spread is always tedious, occasionally boring. The smell baiting helps a little; the buzz of the beer helps more. He muses on the stories he and his father would share, about which country songs were the best at mentioning drinking. Robert always opted for country music. To him, beer was not optional for breakfast but mandatory. A candid man was Dad Robert, amusing also.

Burlin flexes his fingers one more time before lifting the scoped shotgun to his right eye. His body freezes at the same moment his heart thumps in his chest. Shaking his mind of the alcohol-induced cobwebs, he lifts his right finger to tweak the scope into focus. This gesture is out of habit as his weapon has the latest autofocus, high-resolution technology with no human touch needed. The image through the glass is crystal clear. His eye locks in on the most incredible animal he has ever seen.

In the distance some eighty yards away, standing nearly six feet tall at the shoulders, the massive buck raises its head with serious deep eyes that send a chill though Burlin's bones. Just below its left eye is the Z-shaped scar, a confirming tattoo inflicted by the collision with Robert's car windshield seasons ago. The buck stands intently, holding its rack upward in confidence, not unlike a professional athlete who has just taken the field for a major event. The animal is poised, strong, mature, and still.

The hunter is ready for a bounty.

Taking a slow deep breath to temper his adrenaline, the hunter lets his thoughts flow in a relaxed manner. He is looking at the infamous Ben on his own McClusky property, less than a five-minute quad ride from the house. Peering into the scope, he sees the beast move its wide rack from side to side. Burlin views this motion with awe; he is almost humbled by this incredible display of nature. Ben lifts its nose into the air and breathes in a faint trace of musk. Downwind, Burlin sits poised in his blind, holding the shotgun steady as he contemplates the risks of taking a shot. His stomach grumbles from a conflicting reaction to nervous excitement and several beers. Beads of sweat form on his face and fingers. He wants so badly to open the trigger-finger tip on the glove of his right hand, and—crap, what a time to have to pee! The near forty ounces of St. Louis canned brew has oversized his bladder.

∞

Linda steps out onto the deck with its morning coolness, holding her cup of hot tea. She naturally curls her slim fingers around the ceramic souvenir raceway mug, looking out to the edge of the woods. She enjoys mornings like this, and yet she senses some degree of concern, a premonition pushing into her. Linda sips her tea and clears the fear from her head, consciously slipping a hand into her back pocket to confirm her reality on the porch. She convinces herself that the fear is groundless. The sleek teacher is sporting her favorite faded denim jeans with a few bleach-stained tears in the legs. Feeling artistic one day, she had carved these openings in the jeans at random, hoping for a sexy look of soft but fun mileage. Admittedly, but only to her closest girlfriend and not to Burlin, Linda selected a spot just below the left hip pocket to erode the denim. Thus, she shares a two-inch view of her panty-covered cheek to those who dare to look. The artistic action pushes the borderline of sexy versus blatant, yet it gives her a sense of freedom beyond the carefully crafted image of a children's teacher.

She finishes her hot drink, and its fragrance comingles with the lotion that was worked into her skin. Pulling a soft autumn-colored flannel shirt across her breasts, she welcomes the chill of the morning. The cool air surrounds her and counteracts the heat of her arousal. Unfulfilled for a week, Linda lets her fantasies play inside her mind. She purveys the woods, the morning sun, and craves the presence of a male who will satisfy her. It could be a few more hours, but it had already been a few days. She ponders what the day will bring. Where is her lover now?

With a low rumble, a raspberry-colored Ford pickup slows outside of the McClusky homestead. The driver pauses the truck, idling. White backup lights blink on as the vehicle slowly creeps in reverse toward the driveway.

∞

Burlin caresses the trigger up and down with his finger, his vision keenly focused on the target of the huge buck. Trying to keep his hand relaxed, he gently curls his index finger as he keeps the scope zeroed in on Ben. The animal, as if teasing the eager hunter, steps closer over the next few minutes, looking straight at him, leaving his breakfast appetite behind. Ben moves forward—steady, deliberate, and paced. The deer looks at the hunter intently, without fear, and appears to narrow the gap between animal host and prospective killer. Lifting its hooves intentionally and silently, steps turn into feet as the gap shrinks to less than thirty yards. *Thirty yards!* thinks Burlin. The beer keeps backing up. Perspiration continues to trickle and roll down his spine. Ben steps closer. Burlin senses his once-dominant competitive instinct drowned out by nervous uncertainty. Damn it! How stupid could he be in drinking all morning? "Shake it off," he tries to convince himself. "You can do this. Focus, focus, gentle, steady…"

The metal trigger on the Remington feels the mild pressure of a fleshy damp finger. The shotgun recoils with a loud crack, echoing in the woods and sending an alarm of danger to other creatures. The hunter's arms holding the shotgun jerk as the bullet spirals through the barrel and into the once-still air. Burlin knows the instant he pressed the trigger that he had twitched. Unable to sustain a steady shooter's hand any longer, he chose to take the shot and wish the legendary buck down onto the leafy bed of the woods.

As if time is frozen in place, Burlin can swear he sees the deer slug leave the barrel. It's as if he can trace the path of the lead sphere as it zips toward its target. An experienced hunter tries to balance out instincts with skill. He knows immediately that his instincts were accurate, but his skill was off target by perhaps an inch. Big Ben, with instincts of its own, triggers the muscles of its hind legs and raises its body up into the air, stretching some eight feet upward from turf to hoof. By pawing the autumn air with its front feet, the reigning king of the woods snorts out a challenge to the hunter: Game on.

Burlin did not anticipate this reaction, though he should have. Why did he foolishly think that Big Ben would simply stroll into his range and die gracefully with one kill shot? The deer challenged him, and he pulled the trigger. Burlin senses a fleshy snap as the bullet disappears into the body of the buck. The speeding slug did not complete its mission. The instantaneous rearing of the deer altered the impact, and the deer took a hit just below the ribcage. The slug passes cleanly through the flesh of the animal and penetrates a lung. The hunter fails, and now the deer begins to cough up blood, feeling the one-inch piece of metal as it painfully breathes.

Panicking, unable to clear his head to take a second shot, Burlin lowers the Remington. He has no choice now but to climb down from the blind and pursue the deer. Now Ben is going to suffer. How much or how long can only be determined by pursuit.

The huge red deer drops to one knee and quivers, recovering enough to remount all four legs. Ben exhales a steamy pound of heated air. Vapors rise from his nostrils. Ben shakes his majestic antler spread from side to side once, twice, and finally stares at the worried armed hunter.

Ben pauses motionless for a second then coughs loudly, emitting a sound that chills Burlin. The deer attempts to suck in some air but only emits a weaker cough for its effort. With a snort, the deer is able to inhale enough breath to somewhat regain its animalistic composure. Ben trots away from Burlin, who is descending from the tree blind. Burlin thumps to the ground—shotgun strapped to his shoulder—and feels his boots begin to run after the buck. Ben has begun a slow labored gait but gains momentum and picks up the pace, though in pain from the errant first shot. Burlin swings the shotgun into a position poised for a second shot but dares not take it from the rear. Where is the buck going? Confused, the hunter pushes himself to run faster as the deer has already stretched another twenty-five yards between the two with a limping, bounding gait. He senses immediately that the deer is heading out of the woods and toward the house.

The hunter knows as he pursues the animal that he has a problem, one that's branching out like the bare trees of autumn. He can't risk a repeat pull of the trigger. His mind is functioning but blurred from the beers. His chest tightens up from the stress of the failed slug. His puffs of breathing are labored from his trailing of the buck. Regardless of age of the deer or angle of a closing shot, Burlin sees the situation becoming more startling with each second. Past the point of logical thinking, the burly man crosses his gloved fingers in a ridiculous symbol of luck, knowing luck is his only hope of salvaging the situation. It's unlikely he can bring the legend down while chasing and attempting to stay within range. Perhaps the animal would drop or at least falter from the lead wound, and he could mercifully finish it off.

But Ben moves in a direct line from the woods to the house as if being called home. Burlin tries to shake the cobwebs out of his brain, and he continues to lumber afterward. Squinting his eyes, the shooter swears that he sees two figures: shadowed, imperfect images that draw his blurred mind toward another aim with his weapon. The hunter is fading. His steps slowing. His shotgun starting to sag to the ground. He knows the feeling, the circumstances. His mind flips the pages to a decade ago when he had pursued a fleet-footed tailback in college, wearing number 24 on a deep royal-blue jersey with sun-yellow shoulder inserts. Burlin is again chasing the tailback for fifty, sixty yards. The WKU Hilltopper is the last one to have a shot at a saving tackle. Burlin can see vaguely, as if in a fog, the 24 getting smaller with each of his tired steps. Like the tailback, the elusive creature—or whatever the image is—grows smaller and disappears as quickly as a sun ball behind a shadowy hill.

Burlin can't tell if he is running or not, whether he is moving or laying still. He is shaking, chilled to the marrow, sweating profusely, clutching his stressed chest within the heavy coveralls. His lungs are steeled from the rebellion of his heart. He flashes through pages of a lifelong book unopened until now. He had no plans to read it for at least another quarter of a century. Now the odds of nature force the pages of his life before him one by one in a flash-fire sequence. Drifting deeper into pulmonary rebellion, he moves his lips to call out, "Linda, Linda, Lin…" But his words are soundless.

∞

Linda is lost in her own wayward fantasy on the faded deck of the rustic Hoosier home. She is seared with passion; it makes her skin hot from touching. Though the image in her mind is both earthy and beyond this earth, she willingly joins in on the illusion. Her obsessive thoughts morph to a fantasy world where her husband is just an actor, a prop. New imaginary ventures became standing-room-only climaxes. She is smothered with urges on the rain-stained wooden deck. Her self-induced starburst ends abruptly as her nearly closed eyes catch a glimpse of movement in the distance. Linda snaps back to reality as if slapped. Piercing her eyes at the movement from the woods, she focuses on the rapidly approaching creature.

Linda stands against the chill, breathing in the sight of a moving animal. Another creature stirs nearby. A familiar-looking truck moves slowly up the driveway, unseen by Linda. A key is turned. The motor goes silent. A male sporting a brown leather jacket steps from the vehicle, a pistol wedged in his waistband. Angling across the yard to avert detection from his obsession, Darren Henson approaches the distracted wife.

The unmistakable spread of the trophy rack stuns Linda from a distance. "My God." She finds herself gasping. "What the...?" She is mesmerized as the stunning animal—perhaps the legend himself—appears from the woods. The huge buck trots with a twitch. Heavy steam from belabored breathing shoots out from his nostrils. Deep red blood clots frame his gaping mouth. Her eyes remain transfixed; her heart pounds loudly with the realization that Big Ben is racing toward her. The image expands from yards-away smallness to the uninvited shock of the size of the animal as the huge deer gets closer to her with each heartbeat.

The demure female is unaware that her most ominous pursuer lurks just beyond the corner. Henson licks his lips and rubs the ache within his crippled leg. Urges and surges stimulate his blood. He grips the pistol and he too sees the deer aggressively approach the house.

The wounded yet gritty buck gimps Linda's way, steady but with a quiver that labels each step of pain, stopping just yards from the house. The infamous Ben lifts his head and sniffs the cold air, his broad chest stained by a crimson-red blotch that mottled the winter hide of the aging leader. His head moves with a palsy-like jerk, and the rack weighs his majestic face downward toward the brownish grass of the backyard. Emitting a terrifying bellow that echoes from house to woods and back, the muscled red deer follows up the vocal blast with a hacking cough that explodes from deep within the creature's wounded lung. Ben makes a cyclical snap of his head once, twice, and finally, with a third, he lunges forward, expelling a semiclotted mass of snot, saliva, and blood on to the turf in front of Linda. In the middle of the slimy mass is a mushroomed-shaped chunk of metal.

Henson licks his lips and swallows and welcomes a surge of strength in his body. The stalker senses the air, the unfiltered daylight, and the power of his dominion over lesser creatures. His broad shoulders flex. His thighs spring upward as he stretches to his imposing full height. The male steps out into the daylight, injected with a compulsive desire to attack.

Linda is physically stoic, transfixed by the power of the stag and by the shock of her human predator. Ben flares his nostrils as he sniffs. Henson breathes in the fragrance of his own as he lusts after the woman. The abandoned bride reacts as Ben turns swiftly and veers to the right. Henson charges toward her perch on the deck in a maniacal fever. Female adrenaline spears Linda into an aggressive response, converting her fantasy into actions of self-preservation. Reduced to smallness by the enraged and rebuffed aggressor, Linda turns to the familiar prism of the bedroom just as Henson lunges toward the aged rear door of the house. Drawn unwittingly into the deep fight for life, Linda bolts the door, stumbles, and recovers to crawl for Burlin's gun cabinet. It's locked. Linda never shared hubby's fascination with firearms but regretted her abstinence from guns in the instant Henson made his first charge.

∞

The room is cool in spite of seating nearly thirty members of the McClusky clan and Linda's layered family at Hardig

& Schmidt Funeral Home. Another three-dozen local semirural people sit in to pay their last respects to Burlin. Dead at thirty-five, her husband had collapsed as a genetic victim of a heart attack, giving his life doing what he loved: hunting and caring for his sweet college bride, Linda. The widow sits exhausted in the first row, discreetly touching the sleeves on her silk blouse to hide the last remnants of the bruising. She is wearing the gnarled jeans that her late husband found highly arousing. It mattered little to her that her wardrobe display is deemed inappropriate. Burlin would have smiled, smacked her on the ass, and pulled her lithe body into one of his wonderfully suffocating lover's hugs. She senses it to be odd that her freakish desires and fantasies vaporized with his demise. She longs for his touch, his strength, his crude sometimes rough but sincere demeanor—that was all part of his Burliness.

She remembers little of that November morning, only clips and flashes of Ben limping away, of her whirling from the deck and slamming the door shut to avoid the terrorizing advance of the predator. Fearing for her life, Linda retreated to the double windows of her and Burlin's love nest, peering in fear as the rampaging man crashed his feet against and into the back door, shattering it into shards of faded aluminum scraps and broken glass. Henson continued to blast away at the once-secure home, determined to destroy the barrier between him and the petrified woman.

Linda's recollection faded from that moment, perhaps as nature let shock take over or perhaps she dropped into unconsciousness with the man's attack. She later was shown the dropped shotgun, Burlin's favorite heirloom. The Remington had mustered another round. Linda was shown the second slug that had cleanly cut into Darrel Henson's heart from behind, dropping him instantly into a painless and desired quick death. The killer round struck its target at an improbable angle, and Linda was told that the final trigger pull was perhaps Burlin's last act of kindness toward her.

More than one body fell that day; Ben's life ended as well. The local community mounted the legend's antler spread above the crusty yellowed doors of the nearby veterans' hall. Hunters and schoolkids alike admired the majestic trophy, though briefly sorrowed by the price Burlin had paid with his life. The hall is now dubbed McClusky Veterans' Hall.

As the soft and final music ends the funeral service. The jean-fitted widow pauses at the walnut-trimmed coffin with filtered torment. Touching her late husband's right hand for the last time, she curls her forefinger onto his, feeling the cool lifelessness one more time. She reflects on the touches of long ago, real and imagined. Linda pauses by the padded container, drifting into the empty stillness of lost lovers.

Blue Wave

It's another blue day, not the kind of blue that woos one's spirits into a spiral of remorse or longing but, rather, a blue day of nature and of architecture. Blue like the sky, the ocean, the swimming pool, and most everything around it, except for the occasional accents of green imported grass and the brownness of the Camaya Hotel building in Cancun. I sit here on the balcony suite of the aged hotel, which is well-preserved like me, and reflects decades of character. I absorb the immensity of the resort, admiring its cleanliness, maturity, and my spectator's view.

It's easy to ponder the waves of people who flow in and out of places such as this. Hundreds, perhaps thousands, who speak everything from Spanish to Swedish arrive, play, drink, and leave weekly. Each learns that hand motions and facial expressions get you mostly what you need. It's a comfortable place where one can drift away mindlessly into some aura of peacefulness. I find myself floating in and out of that euphoria, the kind where you know that you've floated away to no particular place. I know I was in that magical place twice today already. I don't recognize it until I snap out of it and back to my conscious presence on the balcony. It's a calming feeling, though it makes little sense trying to explain it. Vacationers like me drift away into this nothingness; it's a peaceful void.

Fading in and out, I again scope the classic hotel. The sky is flawless, a hazy pale Mexican blue that stretches left to right until blocked by the rooftops. Shredded cotton clouds, looking lost and lazy, hang up aimlessly some thousands of feet or meters. I wonder if the clouds have accepted the metric system. The sky reaches down to lie flat against the expansive ocean as perfectly as if an artist took a pen and drew a distinct line of demarcation between water and air. The ocean brings animation to each day, layered with moving hues of blue and aqua, the deepest blues reserved for the two-hundred-meter depths of far away. The mighty body of water moves its color palette forward to the shore with alternating blue-and-turquoise stripes. To me it looks like a watery parfait, capped with globs of white foam that look like toppings of whipped cream being licked away by an invisible tongue.

I'm drawn to the pale characters roaming in the aqua waters, overweight and mostly bare. Most sport large beer guts and streaks of sun-stained foolishness, deep pink. Each stands foolishly erect, like bulbous whales bobbing on the ocean until the next lap of pounding water smacks them into a dizzy spin. Eventually, each water tourist struggles awkwardly back to the protective sand of the beach. It's the Wisconsinites, the Iowans, the Slavs, others from across America and Europe who come here to poke fun at the foam-capped waves that sequentially push toward shore. The ocean smirks, aggressively sucking one or two of the white human lugs back with a reverse tide. Its display of force takes most of the water rookies by surprise.

The huge ocean pool is sprinkled with teen boys who are clever enough to duck under the waves, letting the force flow over the top of their skinny backs. Once in a while though, they drink a shot of salty brew through their noses and come up coughing, laughing—claughing. The youngsters seem foolish, playful, and careless, yet the dares of their adolescence are usually not called by the massive ocean. Outnumbering the older slugs three to one, the boys continue to taunt the raging waters with no drain whatsoever on their batteries.

I spot the skinny girls who mingle with the adolescents, most of whom laugh nervously as they pose in knee-deep water, waiting to be hammered by the next wave. Most have the kind of bodies that are not at their peak but soon will be. The periodic photos taken from the shore by their BFFs will be the girls' only reminder of these glory days in the decades to come. The teen boys will get the same treatment by nature as the girls do, just in a different time zone. They too will become older, fatter. The ocean's bevy of splashing spectators is vanilla and chalky, mixed with a bit of pink or deep-red burns. The water does little to coax in the elderly. Where are the old folks?

The color palette diversifies as the white sandy blanket separates itself from the rolling ocean. Dotted on the beach are dozens of wind-worn plastic beach chairs. The chairs are layered with seminude bronzed bodies, torsos split top and bottom with a wide range of hues and patterns of minimally invasive bikinis. If one were to think too much, of which I've been accused, one could separate the younger female set by color: The evenly beige are the midweekers who had time to spread out the solar exposure evenly so they wouldn't look blotchy when they arrived home. These same middlers are parked some distance away from the naive oncers, those who once in every ten years arrive to spend their tax refund on some hot, sunny days on a resort beach. For their money, they burn scarlet streaks on their rippled bodies until they look like the red-and-white round peppermint candies that are given out at the bank back home. The peppermints do have a good time, painful as it may seem, and tend to get themselves into predicaments that make for good stories when embellished back home.

Lastly is the dipped Mercedes crowd, those who can afford to prespray and prepay their excursions to the sunny coast of Mexico. Continually toned, they are greeted as sirs and ma'ams by the staff. Those who remain somewhat humble about their privileged status might even greet the hotel concierge by first name. They have nothing to worry about lying in the sun; in fact, some even think they own the sun. It could be the brownish guy with the laptop on his thighs holding the iPhone to his ear. Maybe he doesn't own the sun yet; he's still negotiating. Perhaps his wife sealed the deal, and he married into money. Now he's managing the sun. Perhaps the swirling wind will flick sand pebbles into his baby computer. Nature has a clever way of evening things out. *Things go in waves*, I thought. It all evens out in the end.

The waves show off now, swirling to a cyclone of water as if a magical chef was whipping the egg-white ocean foam from the aqua liquid. None of the vacationers seems to notice, except me from four stories up. I see the subtle changes and observe the activities, as does the lifeguard. An apparent native, he steps out from underneath a thatched canopy, climbing down three wooden steps onto the hot sand. Beelining for the water's edge, he snaps off two bright yellow pennants from a square wooden post and replaces the caution flags with red. It's a universal language for a jump into the water. Yellow advises to not be stupid, and red clearly conveys that you're on your own.

I continue to enjoy the view, the blue from my perch. The beach is spotted with deep royal-blue umbrellas standing like summery candy-coated mushrooms, not caring if the peppermints are wise enough to use them. The umbrellas are sporadic, splattered across the sand, and they add a pleasant colorful element. Palm trees are randomly plugged into the play area. Each flows gracefully, as if fanning each guest with thin verdant leaves. Most of the umbrellas and palms shade over white plastic scuffed-up recliners and the numerous dog-eared paperback novels. The colors—blues, greens, and whites—go well together. Humankind has a tendency to go for the deeper hues. The pale hues come by more naturally through time, wind, and weather. A tipped plastic tumbler that once held warm Coca Cola rolls in a small circle near an empty lounge chair. I see tourists of various sizes and shapes clicking shots for their social net sites, not realizing that the flatness of a photo never touches the depth of reality. Finally, I see the elderly hidden in the heaviest shade, dozing.

My eyes float to the swimming pool. It's large, roundish, and shallow, unlike the ocean, but it is appealing in its own way. Tiled in a colorful mosaic of dark and medium blues, it sports three connecting circles of some twenty meters each in diameter. Each pool circle comes together to form a large bluish cloverleaf. It's a clever design, one that conveys a wish of good luck but not great luck. If it were wishing guests great luck, it would have four loops, not three. Or so the legend goes. Blue versus green works here, and seven or eight children laugh and splash and throw small balls at parents and caretakers—and at those who care not to partake in noisy pool-party fun. Here the elderly are awakened from their slumber.

The good-luck pool is centered neatly into this tiled cove, nestled between the massive wings of the hotel. The brown-stained stucco walls of the hotel look like worn hands holding the cloverleaf pool. "You're in good hands," the insurance company shared with me on television, but they never offered me a cloverleaf. Not once. But my travel agent did, and here I am fading in and out of nothingness with hours to kill before the next wave of people comes, displacing hundreds like me.

The wind continues to swirl, sucking up the sheer curtains from patio doors left open in the guest rooms. The waterlogged tourists, from the fake ocean to the real one, continue to mill around, many starting to broil from falling asleep while reading half-price mystery novels. A mother in a pink mottled bikini, as ill-fitting as a plastic sandwich bag placed over your hand, squats in the baby end of the pool. She's teaching her screaming two-year-old to "swim." I hear the echo and long for the moment when the heavy wind will cover the sounds of the agonized, land-loving toddler. The swim mom continues, assuming without scientific data that this approach will actually work and that the youngster will soon calm down and become a lovable water dog.

A pensioned couple, here no doubt to get away from their own neighborhood brats back home in Florida, grimace impatiently at both the swim mom and the hysterical toddler. Pulling up their sweat-dampened towels, the retirees vacate the shady hiding spot they've held since ten o'clock. Each gives the mother a scornful look and departs. Mommy smiles sweetly. The non-grandma scowls, and the old lady's husband looks like he's holding in a major fart.

The wet baby screams again from the warm-as-a-bath water, and I swear I hear someone say "shit." Maybe it was the baby, whose diaper looks suspiciously droopy.

The shadow from the two wings of the hotel is a respite from the demon sun. I watch the crowd from above, nestled in my cream-colored lacquered ornamental chair. I'm cushioned with a themed royal-blue pad that absorbs the water from my swim trunks. I feel in control of things: control of life, of health, of the time of day. I drift back into nothingness again, semiconsciousness but not asleep, forgetting for the moment who or where I am. I wonder if I'll be able to recall the effect once I return from it.

Movements of people catch my attention a few feet from the water's edge. There's a circle of flesh, of conservatively clothed people kneeling onto the sand. Four, five, perhaps six or more are down close, each dressed in slacks and polo shirts of the Camaya Hotel's royal blue or of servant's white. What did I miss here? Was it the interim slip into fantasyland or was it the distraction of the bubbling baby a few moments ago? The small circle of hotel workers is lowered on the beach. One body is moving torso high, up, and down while the others keep a protective circumference. One of the squatted members, as if in a séance on steroids, is leaning over from the waist, as if blowing into a—oh no! It's CPR.

I leap up from my steel chair, peering into the bright sunlight to focus on the confirmation of this lifeguard event. There's no question now. A pale male body is lying on the gritty sand as the disciplined rescue workers, both a breather and the chest compressor, continue to do their work. The man is motionless. Music stops. Children pause to see their moms and dads paralyzed at the pool's edge. Some stand up from their seats at the bar while others stare motionless from the beach. All eyes are placed on the recovery team as players rotate to give winded EMTs a breather. A jet ski floats at the shore's edge, painted bright white and green-striped. A burly but serious-looking rider turns off the key.

What happened? I think to myself. *Was it a collapse on the beach?*

My eyes soon conclude that this was an inexperienced wave warrior, who most likely played too close to the powerful water. Overcome by a smashing wave, he was then sucked below surface and into the killing swirls of the undertow. The ocean doesn't have a conscience or a mind. It can swallow each victim whole, with no remorse, and it is simultaneously both an equal opportunity offender and a playful companion.

I stand here motionless, looking down. The waves continue to swirl and pound, alternately circling and rolling up against the wet sand. The rescue party is safety away from harm, still pumping the man's stagnant chest and blowing used air into his mouth. There is no response from the swimmer, who from a distance looks to be perhaps forty years old and easily weighing in at two hundred pounds.

Bodies on the beach stay respectfully away. The team continues to press, press, press, press, and breathe, keeping up the steady cycle and swapping positions. It's surreal. I'm past the point of thinking it's a drill. This is real time. Soon his head will turn. He'll cough, open his eyes, and the lifeguard gets the girl. I had a flashback of some old-fart show where David Hasselhoff runs into the water, probably just two feet deep, and with an incredible camera angle, pulls a lifeless body out of the bay. In a miraculous show of bravery, he breathes life back into the swimmer. All in less than a television minute, thanks to Dave. I remember back home at the city pool. It's a slightly stocky high school girl who guarded the water for nine-fifty an hour.

But this was not nine-fifty an hour. The hour is 1:25 p.m. on a Thursday, and there's no sign of life. I know, because once I came to the realization that this guy's number could be up, I checked the clock. It's been more than six minutes. There's no sputter of the human engine, no coughing like a twelve-year-old would if he got his head pushed underwater at his best friend's pool by his prick-head brother. There's nothing but stillness from the body. Seven minutes. A drab green-shirted man, perhaps five-five, wearing a dark-burgundy cap, runs up to the spectacle with a flat board to load the body of the swimmer. Rotation—press, press, press, press, breathe. How long can he take this? Wake up, damn it! Can't you see these people are trying to help you?

A tall blonde, her hair pulled back into a ponytail and wearing a strapless florescent orange two-piece, walks back and forth near the rescuers. Twice she puts her arms up to her head, hugging herself with her forearms. Her body language looks controlled from a distance. It's as if her arms are trying to soothe her mind, which is silently screaming, "God, this can't really be happening." Oddly, there is no one panicking, no one screaming, and there are no sirens. The only sound is that of the diminishing waves, as each dilutes itself onto the sand, turning the beach color from clean white to a wetted light gray. The wind whistles a bit around the hotel building's edge. Other than that, it is strangely quiet, surprisingly calm.

Is death peaceful like this? Death? I push this morbid thought aside. I find myself flipping through the phases of death made famous by the late Dr. Elisabeth Kübler-Ross: denial, anger, bargaining, depression, and acceptance. Here I am, going through this in the span of what, eight-plus minutes? What am I, a role-player? His life agent? Perhaps others are doing the same thing on behalf of the comatose man. Each of us lives vicariously.

The orange blonde walks back and forth again, her arms warmly sided against her temples. It isn't the hands slapped against the face as in a horror movie but rather the exasperated pleading of a distraught woman trying to wish him back to consciousness. I'm rooting for him, though I know he can't hear me. I'm putting money on him like a derby thoroughbred with twenty-to-one odds. He's going to make his move and take the race—in a time of nine minutes and thirty-three seconds.

But there's no sign of anything from the swimmer's motionless frame. The workers shift him onto the board. Orange blonde is pacing, with forearms still temple-side. The sun buyer has his phone in his hand. He abandoned his laptop and stands by the team. Thank goodness he called. Non-Grandma and Grandpa, having abandoned the crying toddler who pooped her swimsuit and her smiling mother, stand on their balcony. Non-Granny is crossing herself, still a practicing Catholic in her seventh decade. Her husband, the non-grandpa, holds his golfer hat in his liver-spotted hands and bows his head.

I see something, a mask, an oxygen mask, over the mouth of the unconscious vacationer who is still unresponsive, inanimate. "Oxygen. That's good, right?" I say to myself. Nearly ten minutes and he's not on life support. Life support? These thoughts should not be as rapid-fire as they are, shooting at me every second. I'm like the millions who watch scenes like this on their flat screens each night, but this is both slow-moving and quiet. Crying-baby mom is holding her daughter. The little one is silently holding her mom by the neck with no clue at that age what is going on. Mom is no longer smiling. The sun buyer moves back to his chair and laptop. I see a gurney bouncing down the four concrete steps from the left wing of my suite. Oddly, there are still no sirens. Does this mean, perhaps, that it is over? I'm critiquing the team now, my mind saying, *Keep pressing, pressing, one, two, three…*

Each player is trying. One man continues to skip alongside the flat board as the swimmer is carried up to the good-luck pool area. The rescue team lifts the heavy board up two stenciled concrete steps, which imitate random stones. A would-be rescuer is vainly trying to press but looks to be underperforming and clumsy as the team steps up to the pool's edge. The recently arrived gurney is snapped into place, and with an "*uno, dos, tres,*" the pale-white body is shifted to the wheeled transporter. The emergency wagon is unseen, parked at the front lobby on the other side of the hotel wing. The wagon, like the ocean, has no conscience and waits to receive the wave's latest victim. The oxygen mask is clear, no condensation, and with no sign of breathing. Regardless, I cross my fingers, literally cross them, to wish that each moving partner—human and mechanical—does its collective work.

Maybe the swimmer has just drifted into nothingness. Wake up. Wake up!

The fully loaded gurney, bearing the victim is clunked toward the steps to the double doors and ultimately to the marbled hallway toward the awaiting ambulance. A skinny boy, wearing surfer-length flowered trunks, is slung up on top of the gurney. He straddles the comatose, and perhaps lifeless, man, continuing the chest compressions—press, press, press, press—with his thumbs interlocked. The youth firmly pushes with a controlled force that may crack a rib or two but may save a life.

Orange blonde lady, mom, is motioning down the beach. Two pale boys, both displaying a pinkish burn on their shoulders and foreheads, grab flip-flops and shake towels to the wind. The move disperses sand too small for me to see into the air. How calm they seem. Each obeys the admonitions of the woman, who is no longer head-hugging with her arms but is waving the boys over to her. Perhaps the two are a scout and his cub brother. Each complies quickly and silently with no hesitancy. I would never think to grab a towel if my dad were dying from drowning or from being hammered by a four-foot wave. Maybe it's a stepdad or an uncle. Maybe scout boys don't know the gravity of the situation. Perhaps orange blonde mom is keeping them at ease. She's holding up well, all things considered. No more head-hugging. Maybe it's over. Maybe she's in shock. Has she hit the acceptance stage already?

Eleven and a half minutes. My money's no longer on the former swimmer. The skinny kid keeps pressing away as the beach family trails behind, double doors closing behind the gurney. There's nothing more to see. I suddenly feel helpless. Sometimes being respectful is all that you can do. It's twelve minutes, and the gurney is gone. The beach is not empty, but the ocean is void of any vacationing wave splashers. "Hey, it was an accident," the ocean says. "I tried to tell him that I play rough. It's my nature to be wavy. I've been doing this for thousands of years."

The flags on the square poles at the water's edge are still red. They are not at half-mast. The quiet drama is over. Children in chlorine-avoidance goggles climb back into the shallow end of the good-luck pool. Non-Grandma and Grandpa close their patio doors to take a drowning-delayed nap. The peppermints resume their sunny-side-up positions on perspiration-soaked chairs. Sun buyer hugs his woman, and they pack up their poolside belongings, sand-dusted computer, and move toward the lobby. The blueness returns to its place as the key and colorful feature of the waterfront resort, the Camaya Hotel. The ocean continues waving to the now-cautious beachcombers and poolside loungers.

I step back from the patio railing and suck in two deep breaths of gratitude. I nod in tense respect to the ocean. It waves back. I turn and step back into my suite, closing the double doors behind me.

Lying on the fresh sheets, I ponder the event. Swimmer couldn't have suffered. Perhaps a brief panic after the wave took him down. Like most of us, we can't hold our breath for more than a minute. I've tried it dozens of times. Maybe it was a minute-ten when I was a high school athlete, but no more. Drowning is said to be peaceful and calm when you give up hope. Water enters your lungs, and you enter a degree of silent and progressive transition into the next world. Not unlike the nothingness. I hope he didn't suffer. I hope he was revived with no brain damage. I hope. I just hope. I think of the family, the woman in the orange bikini with two boys. I hope that it is not a long and lonely flight home to New York or California or Kansas or wherever. Maybe swimmer is with them, exhausted and grateful.

∞

The brilliant early-morning sun forces its way into my room as I awaken from a dream-filled sleep. I return to the balcony double doors of my suite and swing them open, looking out over the early-morning horizon, the parfait ocean, and the stucco hands of the hotel holding the good-luck pool. I look at the colorful scene and focus my eyes on the ocean waves.

It's a blue wave. And another blue day. Really blue.

Water Baby

The sound is a whistle with wisps of a musical moan. The breeze, somewhat stronger than customary for August, threads through the evergreens, mimics a song that rebounds between peacefulness and eeriness. Lonnie Schmidt senses that the moving air begs for lyrics to its melancholy melody. But he thinks too much. Perhaps it's the artist in him. The breeze chills his skin, offering a contradiction to the sun's rays that filter through the leaves. Rolling his denim sleeves back to wrist length, he sucks in the moment. The scene is mesmerizing from its freshness. The smell of evergreen needles lay carpet-like upon the campground's sandy soil.

The hiker stretches side to side, still achy from the seven-mile hike of yesterday. Castle Peak exhausted him and his wife, Sheri. The popular mount seduced them into climbing its three-thousand-foot ascent during the first half of the trek. She'd done better than Lonnie, stretching her lengthy legs over a wide array of boulders and rocks. He traipsed behind, only able to catch up when an occasional plateau welcomed tired feet. But he got bragger's rights for being the pack mule of the two, lugging a backpack with an assortment of granola bars, bananas, and water bottles.

"So there," the playful hubby had teased Sheri upon reflection around the modest campfire of last night. She pleasantly badgered Lonnie throughout the climb, his frequent utterances of *wow* as he soaked in nature's beauty. Then the words faded to silence brought on by path-weary fatigue. They finished the five-plus-hour excursion worn out. She complimented him for his toughness—and for carrying her luggage. Lonnie retorted by teasing her about the squeal she made on the way back, dipping sweaty feet into the chilly waters of a pond. She fell against her tall husband as she put her socks back on. Though normally as graceful as a swan, her stork-like posture was comical.

The trip to Lake Tahoe was well deserved. Sheri had just been granted partner status at the law firm back in Louisville. The promotion was a reward for eight years of twelve-hour days emancipating abused children from neglectful parents. Unfortunately, most of those "parents" carried their title through biology only. Fully committed to her role as legal advocate and, at times, emotional counselor, Sheri accepted the promotion and, with modest pride, saw her name added to the Web site. Tate, Ponder, and now, *Schmidt*.

"Hey, lover boy! Got time for your girl?" A cheerful voice overlaps the morning breeze as Sheri squeezes Lonnie from behind. "As always, you're deep in thought. Take me with you." Her body shivers slightly from the morning's forty-degree chill.

Lonnie reaches out and pulls her hands into his. "The breeze, the wind. I was caught off guard by how easy it is to hear it singing through the treetops. It's been years since I heard wind in a forest like this. Actually, I don't remember anything like this."

"My, my. You dive so deep at times. Just enjoy it."

"Listen, Sheri. Just listen. It's not just wind, but almost like a song. I hear sounds that are like music, maybe more like the sounds of voices."

"Are they saying, 'Feed me. Feed me?' Lonnie, I'm starving. Let's go eat." With that teasing command, Sheri twists away and turns for the camper, a still-new Artic Fox that is barely dusty. "It's your wonderful imagination again. You always float away, hearing and seeing things that aren't there."

Used to her playful demeanor, he lingers for a moment. "Sheri, I swear it sounds like a child's voice. A baby—crying."

∞

A faded Chevy Blazer rolls into the concrete driveway, its paint mottled and weathered to a patchy blush gray. The tired SUV rattles from too many rough-road miles; it rumbles from multiple corroded muffler leaks. Packed fully, bags of crumpled clothing and dirtied cardboard boxes are crammed against the windows of the car. Following a north-bound curl in the road, the driver steers her worn vehicle from the smooth concrete park entrance onto a graveled path to a remote campsite.

"Ma, can I have more crackers?" The three-year-old boy sucks his fingers and licks in the last remnant of peanut butter from the generic-brand four pack. "I want more. Can I?"

"Yeah, baby. Gimme a sec." The thin thirty-one-year-old curses as she swerves to avoid a pothole, twisting the wheel back and just avoiding the clip of a tree by the front left fender.

Abbey spits out another *oh, shit* as she fingers for the joint that had rolled onto the floor, courtesy of the last road jar. Bumping the steering wheel with her chin, she retrieves the weed with two fingers and returns upright and crams it into her mouth. A flick of her thumb, two sparks, and then a flame causes sweet smoke to billow out the front window.

With lips forced tight around her addiction, the mother curls her free arm into the plastic convenience-store bag. Grabbing another packet, she hands the crackers to her son. "Here ya go, Jaimie. We'll find our way and then we can set up the tent. Would ya like to sleep out in the tent tonight?"

Jaimie shoves a whole cracker into his mouth and mutters a dry "Uh hmm."

The gravelly path roams backward into the woods. The weary mother guides the car past spot after spot of campsites. She responds to a weathered sign marked "Sites

128 thru 145" and weaves through the campground, soon spotting 132. Randomly, she selects this one as her own.

"Here we are, Jaimie. Let momma back up here, and we'll get set up." She likes this spot. It's a nice reprieve from the highway rest stops that they'd parked at over the last few weeks. She and her son have been nomadic since late May, forced out of the mobile home she'd been renting for four and a quarter monthly. While the gas mileage on the Chevy sucks, she finds it cheaper to drive in spurts. The roaming family stopped at rest areas throughout the region and shacked up at the picnic shelters. Abbey is desperate to figure something else out. Now August, it is only a matter of a few weeks before the cold sets in. California is more moderate, and she has rambled farther east than she intended. Tahoe straddles Nevada and settles in for heavy snows starting in September. Vacationing families are home now due to school. With this transition, the money she had begged for disappears.

The door creaks open as she absorbs the site. Crowds are down, so she had picked out this random spot away from the closest tourist. Feeling relatively alone, she ignores the required permit protocol and curls around the hot hood of the car to let Jaimie out. She glances over her shoulder and only sees one camper nearby. There's a Kentucky plate on the rear of a bright silver Jeep Cherokee. A shiny white travel trailer, looking new but not pretentious, sits beside the SUV with windows open and a side awning propped up.

Jaimie hops down and trails his mother to the back of the car. Flipping up the tailgate, Abbey tugs on a garbage bag and rummages until she feels the nylon cover of the tent bag. With one strong pull, the portable shelter pops free from the floor and swings out in her hand. Two plastic bags of clothes follow and drop to the ground. A single two-liter Pepsi bottle rolls and plunks down near her feet. Brown fizz seeps out from the cap rim.

Abbey gathers up an armful of food bags, the tent, and the warm soda bottle and starts the set up. She peels off a flannel shirt, feeling the early heat of the day. The breeze, while still chilly, is no match for the sun. Unzipping the bag, she unrolls the tent and teases Jaimie as to why he's not helping. She asks him to find a rock to hammer stakes into the ground as the tent comes to life. She crawls inside as the nylon stretches to relieve itself from the wrinkles, then sorts out the bedding for the night. Jaimie keeps her warm as they snuggle. She pushes through the contents of a large black bag and pulls out an armful of towels.

Shaking them out and snapping them to stir the air, the mother lays the towels near the back corner of the tent and fluffs them into a loose pile. She stands the Pepsi bottle upright and wriggles it until it agrees to stand on its own. Then she digs into another small bag for her limited food supplies: three small packs of peanut-butter crackers, a bag of salted peanuts, and three jars of baby food. Shoplifting is easy, yet she still needs to ration the food. There are two young mouths to feed.

∞

The Schmidts skip the idea of biking into town, opting for the comfort of the Jeep. Three miles of flat pavement seem mild compared to yesterday's trek, but their mild soreness needs some automotive therapy. The leather seats are a suitable antidote as the couple heads back to the campsite. Their venture today includes an exploration of one of the lakes they passed on a climb and perhaps a picnic lunch. They hadn't been aware of other lakes around Tahoe, just as serene, clear, and cool as the famous lake. Each has its own charm for those who love to meander.

"I'm still amazed at how clear the air is. I'm glad the crowds have thinned out for the school year. I'm glad you could take a break now." The gravel crunches underneath as the Jeep pokes up the pathway. Lonnie glances at Sheri as she too absorbs the serenity.

"Yeah, it's great. The downtime feels good. But I still get twinges of guilt from the caseload…" Sheri's voice trails off as she floats back to the recent cases she was focused on. Oddly to Lonnie, Sheri rarely uses the term *cases* except in the formality of a hearing or courtroom. To her, they are children, kids who are in desperate need of care, support, and in many instances, strong adult guidance.

Sheri is always careful not to divulge intimate details of the goings-on: the reports of beatings, abuse, drug-and bug-infested housing. But she labels each story with a name that makes Lonnie feel drawn in as well. The Jasons, Tylers, Sophies and Amandas, Mias, and Zoes seem familiar to him, as are their traumas. Perhaps she codes the names; it doesn't matter. What matters is that she cares to the point of exhaustion. There is no clear measurement to her effectiveness, only the obsession with saving a child.

"There aren't a lot of campers back here." Always a peruser of license plates, he spots Colorado, Wyoming, and Arizona among the fellow vacationers. California doesn't count, being the host state. He rolls the Jeep up to the camper and spots the two-cloth Louisville Cardinals folding chairs still outside of the fire pit from the night before. Turning in, something catches his eye.

"Ah, we have neighbors." It was more of a question than an explanation.

Casual campers, he notices. The rough-looking Chevy SUV looks more utility than sport. Lonnie senses this vehicle hasn't been much fun over the years. The dull finish and faded plastic grill suggests it is perhaps twenty years old. A woman wearing fatigue as weary as her flannel shirt is carting an armful of supplies from the open rear gate of the car. A toddler sits on the ground of the campsite, drawing random circles on the dirt.

Sheri notices the couple with empathy. The car tag reads California, two months expired.

Lonnie nods as he opens the car door. The new campers barely glance up. There are three or four spots between the two vehicles, just enough to offer a nice woodsy buffer but close enough that in an emergency one could yell for help. She looks like someone of scruffy independence: rough and broke but not asking for anything. At least, not yet. He wonders how well the kid—the boy—is doing. *Just like Sheri*, he wonders.

The Schmidts' venture to Lake Tahoe is for vacation, Lonnie muses. *Let's keep our privacy.* The woman is not sending out vibrations of "Let's get together and do a cookout." They have the luxury of a nice camper trailer pulled with them. The kitchenette and clean toilet suit their lifestyle. They want to rough it? Fine by him. Fortunately, the skinny mother didn't bring a yapping dog to crack the peacefulness of the woods. The wind-voice of this morning seeps back into his mind. The sound—an earthy, childlike utterance— draws him again. Is it the wind? He feels nothing but senses everything.

The boy picks his nose and continues to stroke his circle. Sheri wants to give him a bath.

∞

"Now you just set here. Momma's goin' to get us something to eat." Glancing back, she reaches over to pat Jaimie on the top of his head and turns off the ignition. "Thank God," she whispers. "He ain't got lice." She'd scrubbed him down a few days ago at a McDonald's off Route 80, even rinsing out his stained Superman underwear in the sink. Ignoring the glare from a customer, a half-minute stare-down that was as dirty as the shorts, she finished the bath-and-laundry gig in less than ten minutes. Buying the two-for-fifty-cents apple pies and a large Coke before leaving, the nomadic family hits the road again. The aimless wandering got her here with no plan except to survive.

Now she needs to be careful. Tahoe is sparsely populated, and the air is healthy but reeks of money. Thinking she can do a quick grab and go, Abbey notices there hasn't been a cop in sight since she rolled in yesterday. Unmarked cars, perhaps? She knows she can garner a few bucks here and there, but right now, she needs food.

"Just lay your head down, Jaimie. Pretend we're playing hide-and-seek. But don't you let no one tap on the window or spook you. I'll be back in just a minute with a *donut* for you."

"Jelly?"

"Jelly. Just like you like it, baby. Now lay your head down and cuddle up till I get back." With that command, Abbey—mother, driver, petty thief, and vagabond—pushes open the creaky door. Hitting the lock button, she steps toward the bakery. Its neon-red light fuzzes the scripted word *Open*.

Jaimie rolls down onto the backseat, curling up against the warmth. The three-year-old shoves his grubby thumb into his mouth and sucks, longing to be coddled. Shifting against the rough cloth seat, he settles his head into a bundle of towels and reaches his left hand into the folds. His fingers seek out the curl of another small hand.

∞

"Love this wine. Your good taste always amazes me." Sheri lifts the plastic goblet graciously, glancing through the curve of the glass to enjoy the deep purple of the Cabernet.

"I bought it because of the label," Lonnie confesses. "The cluster of grapes looks a lot like the canvas I sold to Winnow's Winery in Bardstown last year. Maybe I'll give this place a call and introduce my artwork. It will let me branch out." He chuckles at the pun.

"That's a tasteful idea," Sheri echoes back. With this second bottle, the buzz is setting in. Sheri rarely drinks wine, perhaps a sip or two at a business function or fund-raiser. But the nighttime air, the popping fire, and the chilliness of the California-park night lull her into consumption. Both get giddy during the rare times when they hit bottle number two. Silly humor takes over the conversation, and the blissful couple floats down a stream of teasing that makes her client children seem as far away as his paintings back home.

Draining his glass with the taste of a last drop, Lonnie reaches over and tosses a splinter of wood into the fire pit. A splash of sparks floats up. Heated fireflies drift then fade quickly away. The bright glow of the embers darkens the woods around them. There is another crackling sound, a howl in the distance, and the rustling of leaves from a growing breeze.

"Chilly?" Lonnie's eyes roam over Sheri's curves, hidden by a blanket and two layers of sweatshirts. Her legs are curled up within her jeans. She's still gorgeous after all these years, more than a dozen since they first met. This week is their tenth anniversary; and Tahoe, the reward. Good wine, the glow and aroma of a campfire, and filtered by the tree, a breathtaking array of stars smattered throughout the sky. A suddenly cold wind whisks across his face. He shudders.

"Yes, a bit. Normally the wine would heat me up. Maybe I'm tired. It's been a fun, busy day. I'm still on Kentucky time. It feels like midnight." She stifles a yawn and shifts in her camp chair. "I think I'm going to call it a night."

"I'll come in a sec." The artist hates to waste a good log or a ripping fire. Though not much of a camper, he craves the outdoors and soaks in more of the relaxation. He carefully kicks the last log, causing it to tip further into the coals. Sparks light up the air in front of him. The temperature is dropping, the mountain air overcoming the fire's admirable efforts to heat the campsite. The breeze picks up speed as it swirls around the RV. He wraps his arms around his sides for a temporary reprieve from the chill.

Lonnie is drifting, sinking into the quietness of nature's cocoon. Being mesmerized by this ambiance is great, but odd how he doesn't recognize it until he snaps back to reality.

And snap he does. He hears the voice again. The wind? No, surely not. The perceptive man hears the subtle, distinct voice of someone crying in the wilderness. It's the campfire, the whistle of the breeze. His imagination, Sheri had said yesterday. It's nothing really. Nothing more than nature and the artist's own imagination together, swirling around the campsite. He had been out of the city just a few days, forgetting how many noises there are in the woods.

There it is again. A soft whimpering, childlike. Lonnie listens intently, filtering out the distracting sounds of the fire and the pleasant noises of Sheri settling inside the camper. The sound of a voice lifts, floats, and them settles again. He absorbs it. It is the delicate sound of a voice, lonely and desperate.

A baby.

∞

Abbey shifts in her sleep. The hard ground presses into her hips in spite of the thin layer of pine needles beneath the tent. Immune to her own body smells, she curls her arms around Jaimie's tiny body and feels him breathing deeply against her. Having awakened for the third, perhaps fourth time, of the night, she is shivering more from the nightmares than the cold. The climate evolves quickly as early autumn commands attention from campers. Abbey had only recently thought of this. Body heat and a thin blanket layered over her and her son are the only respites from the deepening cold.

The nightmares are vivid and a hindrance to much-needed slumber. She lays silently in her own thoughts, hoping to sleep off her vibrant storm of fears. She has trouble sorting out the measure of exaggeration within each episode. The haunting rubs her mind, and she has a difficult time discerning if she is sleeping or awake. *Abbey, are you certifiably crazy?* she wonders. On and off of a full menu of prescriptions over the past few years, she retains a blurred vision of reality. She knows she is in Lake Tahoe, that she is a mother. Her recollections are of better but not cheerful times when she and Jaimie had lived in an actual home. A cheap manufactured box yet still a home.

Images flash in front of her and don't stop there. Each image attacks her, stabbing her mind with shooting volts of current down through her heart and then onto her back. There are faces on the tiny bodies, round cherubs with chubby cheeks and toothless smiles that drool on her lips. There are two babies, not twins but similar in some ways. Each is new to the earth, not fresh born but settled in as much as young babies can be. The siblings, one a pale girl and the other a meatier boy with hints of a swarthiness and tightly curled hair, spin one after the other in the worrisome cloud of Abbey's dreams.

d.o. allen

The babes shoot forward rapidly toward Abbey's face, mimicking a ninety-plus-mile-per-hour baseball with arms and legs attached. With no sound but a coo, each one stops, smiles, and evaporates as quickly as she or he had appeared. Like shooting stars, each burns out before striking the distraught mother's earth heart. The apparitions come and go frequently at night and in spurts during the daytime hours. The babies are naked and not afraid, perhaps mature beyond their infancy. Abbey knows the faces but dares not reach out to either child. Once they had names. She doesn't remember exactly. Even in a torment, they are part of her. Abigail? Abilynn? She vaguely remembers the name of one. The daughter appears before her, innocent and yet haunting.

Shifting in her restlessness, Abbey curls her arms tightly together, missing the comfort of a pillow that once belonged in her bed, bugs and all. She has visions of pillows, some three or four feet wide and colorless but not transparent, billowing toward her face. Drawn toward the huge cushions, she longs to smother her face into the folds until she can no longer breathe. The pillows have no human life beyond their silklike covers but remain floating in the air until she literally turns toward the beckoning cushion and leans in to it. The feeling is one of seduction, wooing, drawing in. Then a vacuum sucks the air out of her lungs until she gasps awake, terrified and screaming.

One sequence of night sweats had her head being smashed by a grave marker. Its bronze hardness crushed her teeth and bloodied her mouth and, after striking, paused in front of her wounded face. "Read me," the marker said, animated in her terror. "Abilynn Jaide Taylor. May 2, 2009 to September 13, 2009." Abbey screams, *No, no! It wasn't my fault!* The marker demands acknowledgement; the haunted mother complies.

A stab of pain permeates her lower back; she juts awake from another horror flick. A cry is heard; Jaimie awakens with a taunting moan. Abbey shifts her weight, only to see her knee pressing against her son's small hand. Tears erupt—almost explode—out of the once-sleeping toddler's eyes as he attempts to wriggle his fingers free from the pressing weight of his mother. More crying then whimpering.

"Oh, shit! Baby, baby, Mom's so sorry. I had a nightmare." Huddling close, Abbey gently takes his limp arm and begins a massage across his pained but not broken fingers. His near screams are stifled by her bosom with a tightness that nearly causes another episode of pain.

"You'll be all right. I'll be more careful. Jaimie, Jamie, my baby."

With boyish familiarity, the youngster sobs, wipes his snotty nose against her chest, and is soon asleep. Abbey feels his heat, his sweat, and releases the pressure from her hug. Darkness subsides inside of the tent. Her eyes adjust to the grayness of the night, less black than before. Heavy breathing lifts the chest of her son toward her own beating heart. She hears soft crying. *Another dream*, she ponders, perhaps less stressful than before. Will it be Abilynn again? Please, no pillows. No markers. *Please, baby, come to mommy. Mommy loves you.* The night creeps come again. A baby cries, a mother weeps, and a toddler sleeps, fingers curled in dulled pain.

∞

Another wild nightmare drifts into the tent. A disturbed mother is drawn into the horrific scene once again. Abbey sweats through the psychological scenery that flicks from baby to pillow to grave marker and back. A baby boy this time, taking his turn at zipping toward her, stopping just inches short of her mouth. He smiles coyly then abrupt retreats. "Aaron Paul," the baby's lips seem to say. Aaron Paul. Aaron Paul Taylor, Abbey fills in the blank as if commanded by the six-month-old specter. She once knew the details, the dates, but it's now a smudge upon her memory, a stain on her conscience. Was it 2012? Not long ago. June-ish something. Maybe the twentieth or so. Not even two years ago. No, less than that.

Aaron Paul zips toward her again with a smile that replicates that of a youngster's glide down a park slide. A playground slide, yet at thirty miles an hour. His chubby face speeds toward her and locks in a quarter inch from her face, as it has hundreds of times before. Abbey hears a gurgling, a gasp. Her face is splashed with water as the baby spews out a lungful of clear liquid that smells of chlorine. Aaron Paul's skin fades from a blackened cream to a gray blue as he expels the last drops. He is catapulted backward by an invisible bungee cord and into a body of water, a pool with pale-blue flowers embossed on its vinyl liner. The water playground is alluring and cold. Abbey is mesmerized, drawn forward and downward until she is suspended just above the water's edge.

The pool reflection pierces her eyes, though there is no sun. She lets her eyes first skim the surface and then she stares deeply into the depths of the water. The lapping water distorts her perspective, yet the image of the plaque below is apparent, chilling. Is it a foot across, maybe more? The rectangular shape is familiar. The grave marker lays settled on the bottom. The inscription is blurred but legible: "Aaron Paul Taylor. January 20, 2012–June 30, 2012."

Abbey twitches upward, legs curled under her as she shivers from the fear-inducing nightmare. Her head pounds with the vision of the boy, the pool, and the haunting grave marker. She begs for clarity and a degree of sanity. Or better yet, a fix. The tormented mother no longer can separate sleep from waking hours. The dark and terror-inducing videos haunt her constantly no matter what she is doing, a sticky shadow that plays twenty-four hours a day.

Wiping a dirty sleeve across her forehead, she fans the shirttail out to cool herself. The damp shirt is then discarded. The tormented mother breathes in the dank air of the canvas, soiled clothes, and her own body odor. Starving for anything to provide solace, she curls her fingers around the flannel shirt and fluffs it into a pillow for Jaimie. Pressing it underneath his snoring body, she kisses him on the cheek. His cherublike face sputters. A bit of drool slides down his bottom lip.

Abbey inhales deeply, sucking Tahoe air into her lungs. For an instant, she reflects on the peace of long ago, before Aaron Paul and Abilynn, before the incessant wailing and the snotty noses and constant kid puke. Before the pathetic aftereffects of her reckless nights with strangers. The times when warm naked flesh meant more to her—at least for a few hours—than anything but illegal and self-abused drugs. She creates what she doesn't remember, fills in the darkness with images that are better than history.

The reprieve lasts but a few minutes. The whimpering starts again, this time for real: a snorting inhale and a sobbing hiccup jab Abbey's ears. The sounds spill into her mind once again. The baby is just a shadow next to Jaimie, wriggling her legs in the darkness. Still quivering from the cold, Abbey avoids covering her ears with her hands and instead peels off her remaining top. Instinctually, she reaches for the tiny body nestled at the edge of Jaimie's ruffled bed of blankets. Lifting the baby, naked but for a dampened diaper, the mother draws the baby to her breast.

The scene is sober, regimented, and without compassion. A mother-and-child reunion of the worst kind: heartless. The baby suckles. Mommy succumbs to another nightmare, to her shadowed world again. Time reverses itself with Aaron

Paul curled in her arms. The toddler is whimpering. *Again*. Abbey steps closer to the pool's edge and, kneeling down, lets her arms drop into the water. Baby Aaron bubbles, bobs, and is quiet. The mother presses her right hand onto the baby's chest and watches the bubbles fart out of his mouth as his image becomes slurred. Aaron releases downward, lulled down by a watery gravity. His mother watches like a complacent spectator. Abbey keeps her kneeling position at the pool's edge, reflecting on the similar death of her daughter three years before. The flashback is a nightmare within a dream, a layering of reality with horror.

∞

Sheri's coffee mug heats her fingers as she steps into the filtered light of the morning. Dust particles float downward among the tree branches, remnants of the dirt cloud stirred by a park ranger's truck moments ago. The white Chevy SUV sported a heavy dark-green stripe and the California State Parks logo, complete with a strolling bear, pasted on its doors. The ranger paused, exiting his vehicle to check the lodging tag posted on her and her husband's, Lonnie's, campsite then moves on. As she sips the coffee, she glances but doesn't notice that he failed to spot the smallish tent and rustic car of their immediate neighbors. Are they squatters? Perhaps, she concludes. Perhaps.

There's a gnawing concern within her that maybe there *is* a baby inside the travel-worn tent.

Still, there were never any *visible* signs of another infant among the twosome, at least not to her awareness. Her husband's always-active imagination is convincing. She pricks her ears to listen. No wind this morning. A few birds chirp an early-morning sonnet. A sound, a murmur? Perhaps a whimper from a baby? Maybe, just maybe.

"Crap, Lonnie! You freak me out when you do that!" His cool morning hands wrap around her ribcage, followed by an armful of hug. Admittedly lost in thought, she is chastising him more for breaking her listening concentration than for the physical start he had given her.

"A crime of opportunity," Lonnie confesses. "And you're so close and yet so far away. In a beautiful setting like this, where were you? Hopefully, not at work."

"An odd lady—the transient. Did you speak with her?" Sheri sips her coffee, not much warmer now than her skin.

"Not really. Just a nod, a safe acknowledgment from the edge of the road."

"And the boy?"

"Still there. I saw them both hop in the car. The mom, I presume that's what she is, had him crawl up into the backseat of the clunker. Didn't look like she strapped him in. What struck me as weird is that she went back to the tent and came out holding some kind of bundle. It shocked me at first, as though she was smuggling something out of a store. Then *zap!*" Lonnie taps his temple for emphasis.

"Zap, what?" Sheri queries, having lost interest in her mug.

"Like zap in that she does have a baby with her. What else could it be? A stolen puppy?" Lonnie's eyes scan the distance. "I should go over there and check it out. Why hide a baby? There's no point in it unless…"

"Don't even think that way." Sheri's instruction is easy to bark out, but she questions her own command. Children are her clients, she reminds herself. But how far does her concern go, from Louisville to Lake Tahoe? No longer in vacation mode, she is critically thinking *what if*? There's some meat to Lonnie's ponderings.

A gravelly sound distracts them as the ranger's Chevy hums by. A nod and a wave—have a nice vacation—and he is off to his next venture in the thousand-plus-acre playground.

A stomach growl urges Sheri back to the camper. Her nudge of Lonnie turns him around as well.

"Tomorrow. Tomorrow, I'll say something," Lonnie promises, though she looks at him skeptically. Sheri is now in the camp of plausibility. Is there a baby, another child? Sheri feels the urge to respond to her own conscience and drop a suggestion herself at the ranger station.

"Damn it, Lonnie, if you're wrong."

Sheri clatters the griddle down onto the range and ignites the propane stove. Hotcakes are the order of the morning, along with sausages and muffins. She and Lonnie trade off on the chef role with no particular pattern as to who or when. Her stomach makes an uneasy quiver as she wets the batter with milk. *This is sentry duty now. He's the lookout. I'm logistics.* Never before had she been so enamored with keeping tabs on someone else like this.

Lonnie has turned and flipped apart the miniblind slats of their RV. *May as well keep watching.* And he does.

∞

The rip in the tent is a reminder of Abbey's rage last night as she cursed the demons within her. Not once can she recall escaping the horrific nightmare or, for even one moment, actually sleeping. Could it be that she lay fitfully in pain all night, counting the insect chirps from outside and inside the tent? Her mind was hammered with replays of babies past and present, toddlers here and then.

The pillow—oh God, the pillow! Alone, it streaks at her as large as a door, smelling of a child's skin after a warm bath but coming at her face like a feather-stuffed tsunami. The billowing threat rushes at her, pausing an inch away from her face and then rebounds backward, just as Aaron's face had appeared many times prior. She coughs from a lack of oxygen and gasps for air. Her mind shudders in fear of being suffocated. Awakening from the garish dream, she had found her arms flailing in the air, hands clawing at the vacuum once filled by the satanic pillow.

This is more than a nightmare. She swears it is real.

The face is next, always next, as Abilynn flies toward her larger than life to where her breath can be felt on Abbey's lips. Teasing, taunting, and aggravating, the little girl's image speeds back and forth, never touching and yet never evaporating either. Ten or twenty times—who knows how often?—this rapid-fire facial image comes toward her. The conclusion rarely varies. The pillow returns and is the last smothering scene she experiences before consciousness.

Last night petrified her, an unexpected alteration within the horrific ordeal.

There were letters, a marking of words. Abbey sees her own quivering hand writing with a thick blood-red marking pen. Letter by letter, the message appears. For the first time ever, the huge ominous pillow bears a message like that of the grave marker:

"Abilynn Jaide Taylor. May 2, 2009 to September 13, 2009."

Abbey's torture continues as flashes of the past resumes. Abilynn lay sleeping innocently, her chubby, four-month-old body curled against the corner of the mobile-home bedroom. The near hour-long ordeal of screaming had left the infant exhausted and unfulfilled. The baby wears only a diaper and an oversized faded Dora T-shirt, a two-dollar bargain from Walmart. Her fingers twitch as she rests. Her skin is damp from the fitful crying of moments ago. Her mother, Abbey, sits on the edge of a floor-dwelling mattress less than five feet away. Abbey is tired, irritable, and strung out. The last in a sporadic trail of men has just left the dilapidated aluminum trailer. The few dollars in her jeans pocket did not come from any of the nameless guys.

She is too tired to care or to charge for her affection. The exchange is for drugs, anything that pushes her mind out of this dump. Abbey is not even sure if one of her visitors is Abilynn's father or not. Who really cares? She is a weary mother, a pathetic soul, and driven to drive—away from here, away from kids, away from this tick-infested mattress. She's been through this before. The nightmares, the sniffs, the snorts, and the needles. The emaciation of hunger and the overbearing weight of caring for a kid whom she doesn't want.

She had loved once, truly loved, and had received the same in return from a soldier, Preston Whooley. He'd stuck with her for a year or more. Never was there more of a week's gap between video Skypes and phone calls. That is, until the roadside bomb, an improvised explosion in Iraq, shredded his body.

Their emotions were deep and caring, the lovemaking tiring and satisfying. The sergeant, a muscular African American who'd been in the army seven years, had seeded her. The baby, a wonderful and healthy boy, was born three months after he was deployed. Abbey heard the news of Preston's death in a phone call from one of his war mates. The message was brief. She didn't even remember the caller's name, only that he was a lieutenant, and Sergeant

Whooley—"Pres"—had died a hero. Unmarried and left with nothing, Abbey, in many ways, died too. The surviving son, Jaimie, holds a warm place in her heart. Darkly handsome, the boy is her only solace within her now-miserable life.

Abbey leans forward and takes a pillow firmly in her hands. Slipping to her knees, she crawls over to the corner of the room, rubbing against the soiled and dog-shit-stained carpet. Eyes glazed and head spinning, she lifts the pillow inches away from the sleeping Abilynn's face and pushes down firmly. There is no sound, no movement, except for the shaking of Abbey's arms as she applies pressure.

∞

Tapping his password into the cell, Bob Cranick murmurs how the fingerprint mode never works to allow him to make calls. So it is back to the old-fashioned way—9723 as the screen smiles to life. Icons and apps glow stoically in front of him as he rolls down Alpine Meadows Road. A park ranger for seventeen years in the Tahoe area, he is checking a follow-up voice mail from the office.

On an otherwise quiet and beautiful morning, Cranick received a report from a camping couple, the Schmidts. The Schmidts had permitted their RV to campsite 244 a few days ago. The wife, who according to the dispatcher is a child-advocate attorney, had stopped in to convey a concern. Not an accusation, mind you, but a concern for a baby who needs looking into. Sheri, the attorney, had not openly stated there was anything wrong, only that her husband had heard the sporadic sound of a baby crying. Oddly, neither she nor her husband, Lonnie, could actually see if there was a baby there. They had only seen a haggard-looking woman of some thirty years and maybe a hundred pounds toting a three-year-old boy.

But the bundles, the sneakiness of the woman, perturbed the couple. Could someone check it out?

The state-park protocol still required that all calls be recorded, but when a walk-in occurred by a well-meaning camper, there was no formal trail of communication, only passing of the word to the roaming ranger on duty closest to the scene. Most calls came into the California office, which covered the largest of the camping region, versus Nevada's boundary. Cranick is opening up his phone when the dispatcher's voice sharply stings his ears. "Mobile Unit 12, switchover" come the instruction from the nervous dispatcher.

A switchover is never good. The simple admonishment means a sensitive call has come in, one that needs to be handled with discretion and away from the public's hearing. Cranick does as he is told and clicks the button on the radio to a nonpublic band. As he listens, he stomps on the gas pedal of the heavy SUV and rumbles out onto the main road, stirring up dust. The emergency-light bar comes alive with the flick of a switch, and his speedometer needle presses to the right. "Come on, come on," Cranick curses, and it seems to take forever to get to the seventy-mile-per-hour limit authorized in a code-three call.

He guesses, in his experience and excitement, a three-mile ride to the campsite and perhaps another twelve to fifteen minutes at a near sprint to get to the trailhead. He presses his foot hard against the rubber mat. The truck is floored but finally responding to the command, *Speed up.* The trail, a rugged but popular one during peak season, leads to the first of two small lakes that are nestled into the rising hillside. First-time hikers are surprised to discover other clear cool lakes dot the landscape, like nature's stepchildren to the larger and more magnificent Lake Tahoe.

Cranick projects thirty minutes to get there, prays for considerably less.

∞

"Another wow!" Lonnie exclaims, glancing in a circle at the wonderful cluster of trees as the trail snakes upward. "I thought I had used them all up, but there's always more to see." Thirsty after the six-hundred-foot rise in the needle-padded pathway, he swills down three gulps of Gatorade.

"Impressive, but after an hour of uphill trekking, my feet are sore." Sheri's pink running shoes have a beige hue from the dust and scuffling of feet since their departure from the campsite. "Isn't there a lake back in here somewhere close? I'd like to soak my feet. The cold water will feel good."

"Yeah, the phone signal is fading, but I think it's got to be close. But I thought that yesterday. Each stopping point is farther away than we think." Lonnie forgoes a manly bravado and, admittedly, could use a break himself. "Did you notice that the mom and her kid are gone? I heard some rustling around daylight this morning. Heard the engine fire up, and she took off crazy fast. Left her tent behind, torn open like it had been sabotaged."

"It figures. But maybe a bear scare or something? Or she got spooked by the ranger?"

"Not sure, and it was too dark to see who all left. The kid and her, but I couldn't tell if there was anyone else. It was too dark." Lonnie had waited an hour or so till the light came up before exploring the abandoned campsite. A few ruffled blankets, remnants of granola wrappers, and a kid's sock or two. Nothing much.

The couple falls back into silence as they trudge forward, their feet scuffing the pine needles and occasionally kicking a rock. The air is fresh and crisp in contrast to the stickiness of their bodies. The trail is isolated. The lake comes into view as first a dark line on the horizon then a blue pool of water, much larger than expected. The lake draws them immediately with small lapping waves that wash up against small eroded pebbles.

Lonnie and Sheri pad across from the filtered shade of the forest pathway to the open beauty of the lake's edge. Lonnie quickly kicks off his shoes and strips off the socks, feeling stone jabs underneath a sole as he steps toward the welcoming water. As he glances back at Sheri, his thoughts are on a foot-first splash into the coldness. Her Nikes are already discarded. She is just an arm's length away, keeping pace with him and taking on an almost sprinting pace.

Their joy is short-lived as they brake to a sudden stop.

Is it a…?

Lonnie glances out into the water and sees a quiver, a ripple. The pale, grayish form is barely two feet in length. The water puffed up the diaper of the baby, now face down, and its tiny arms. Feebly, it makes a weakened wave into the coldness of the lake. The would-be rescuer high-steps farther into the lake, still shallow after ten yards. Sheri shrieks as she reaches into her shorts' pocket to retrieve her cell phone. Begging for reception, she nervously fumbles for the keypad to open up the security.

Arms dripping, Lonnie splashes forward toward the shoreline, cradling the tiny water baby in his left arm, leaning his head down toward the baby's mouth. Sheri's voice quivers as she screams into the phone, "Nine-one-one. Who is this? Can you…What? Can you hear me?"

Leaning onto the loose sand, Lonnie strips off his shirt and cushions the baby, whose mouth is a gap, a tiny round toothless oval. The color remains grayish. Fingertips are just turning blue on the baby's tiny hands. The resuscitation effort continues. Lonnie reminds himself to be gentle and begins three-fingered compressions onto the baby's chest then leans forward to breathe both air and hope into the chilly body.

"Yes, no! It's about an hour into the trail. What? I can't hear you." Sheri's face is pale as she struggles and stammers into the phone. She swirls about forward and to the side, glancing at her lifeline for the best possible signal.

"… on their way. Stay on …" A voice pops from the speaker slot. Sheri's hand shakes violently as she watches Lonnie perform his best to breathe, press, press, press. The color bars on her phone, drained by the use of a global tracking during the hike, are staggered red on her screen.

She faintly seems to hear something about a ranger close by, on his way.

Lonnie is still kneeling—breathe , press, press, breathe.

Sheri prays out loud, "Please, God. Please. Please. Please."

More breaths come, more compression, still gentle, onto the infant's chest. Lonnie stretches his back and arches upward, refreshing his spine for the next phase of his lifesaving attempt. Leaning in again, he feels his lips cover over the tiny mouth. He blows in halfway. The effort mimics a soft sigh, an exhale after a long day, yet it has only been minutes. He is tiring, as much from the anxiety of perhaps losing the baby as from the awkward posture of his commitment to revive the baby.

Sheri clings to the phone, silent now and losing life itself as the energy saps from the cell. Her face turns upward toward the warm morning sun, lips trembling with unspoken words. Still holding the now-helpless device to her ear, she kneels down next to her heroic husband.

Morning breezes whistle through the pines, and a near-silent wave claps near a husband and his wife, baby beneath the man's lips.

A slapping sound is heard, paired with gasping, as the sprinting ranger runs the remaining sixty yards to the lakeside. Cranick sheds his bulky belt and hat and shouts instructions into the static-filled mobile radio. Panting now, he sprints the gap between himself and the couple, now a trio, and begs for wisdom and a helicopter.

As Sheri covers her ear with a lifeless phone and her mouth with the other hand, Lonnie continues to beg and breathe, beg and plead. His exhales send another wisp of air into the small lungs of the still-wet baby.

Cranick collapses to his knees beside the couple, near breathless, and takes the baby's hand gently into his. The fingers are cool. He turns the hand over and fingers for signs of life.

Lonnie lifts his mouth away from the baby and sees a quiver from the naked chest. Turning the child onto his side, there is a cough, a gurgle, as clear water trickles out of a small blue-lipped mouth.

A whimper. Sounds carry up into the wind. It's the voice of a crying woman who longs to hold the innocent baby to her breast. The wind lifts up the sigh of a weary and relieved man, thrilled by the baby's movements. A park servant's voice is heard again, sending directions to the rescuing team.

And the water baby cries.

Insights from the Author on *The Die*

I'm pleased that several of my stories are included in other books, including several anthologies and university publications. Here are insights behind selected stories from a previous book *The Die*. I enjoy hearing your thoughts on my writings, so please share them with me.

Many of us can sympathize with Karl, the lonely widower in "The Die." As the story unfolds, however, you will discover that grief has a dark side. This story was chosen as the title for this book as many people were drawn into and captivated by the story.

"Mall Train" describes the worst possible fear of a parent—the kidnapping of a child. The story still gives me chills when I read it. You may never go to a shopping mall again without thinking of Madison in this thriller.

"Shadowbox" somewhat mirrors a lifelike setting you may have imagined. You soon sense where the story is headed but are surprised at where you end up.

"Last Ride"? Who of us hasn't had a fleeting fear of an accident with an amusement-park ride? I let my imagination go with Clay's anxiety and played out both his fears and, perhaps, yours. "Sometimes you just need to let go."

A trip to Barcelona, Spain, sparked the idea for "Angel de Oro," a lighter story with a theme of romantic intrigue. The street performers of this wonderful city are colorful and entertaining, so I imagined *what if.*

Coming Soon from *d. o. allen*

Canvas

More suspense in small doses from the Story Painter.

The blotch is a brilliant red spot on the floor. Embarrassed, the young student quickly stoops down to dab it up, hoping no others caught the accident. Blood red. Anna Mae cringes at how eerily similar the stain looks to her monthly period. She shivers, being timid and somewhat weak, and smears the paint with a wrinkled cloth that shows every color but white. Her clumsiness is not infrequent. Always jostled by the abrasiveness of her college professor, she is a frequent and notable star on this classroom stage. With such a modest class size, there is no place to harbor her fears in the shadows of this decades-old art room.

She longs to blame it on her cloistered background. Her awkwardness is perhaps a by-product of this rapid thrust into secular college life. The young girl argues with herself, whether or not she has a predisposition to cower to dominant personalities. The resulting nervousness leads to her slips, trips, and falls.

Added to this are the dropsies, those shticks, those freakish acts when she looks for the deep black hole to crawl into. She senses the snickers behind her back, though no one smiles on the surface. Other students lay low for fear of being openly mocked by the instructor. Glancing at her pallet, Anna Mae stares at the dab of raven-black acrylic and imagines there is enough paint to actually create a hole onto—into—the floor. Then whoosh, *like water down the drain, the girl can sink into the void where she is free from humiliation.*